Relics of a Saint: A Barbados Mystery

Trevor Gibbs

◆ FriesenPress

Suite 300 - 990 Fort St
Victoria, BC, V8V 3K2
Canada

www.friesenpress.com

Copyright © 2021 by Trevor Gibbs
First Edition — 2021

All rights reserved.

No part of this publication may be reproduced in any form, or by any means, electronic or mechanical, including photocopying, recording, or any information browsing, storage, or retrieval system, without permission in writing from FriesenPress.

No part of this book may be reproduced, stored in a retrieval system, or transmitted in any form or by any means electronic, mechanical, photocopying, recording or otherwise without prior written permission of the author in accordance with the Copyright Act.

Any person or persons who do any unauthorized act in relation to this publication may be liable to criminal prosecution and claims for damage.

While the story and characters in this book are totally fictional, the background historical information has been gathered from several sources, detailed in the bibliography at the end of the book.

ISBN
978-1-5255-9076-4 (Hardcover)
978-1-5255-9075-7 (Paperback)
978-1-5255-9077-1 (eBook)

1. FICTION, MYSTERY & DETECTIVE, HISTORICAL

Distributed to the trade by The Ingram Book Company

Table of Contents

CHAPTER ONE Wrecking Ball — 1

CHAPTER TWO Ladies' Man — 11

CHAPTER THREE Mysteries — 31

CHAPTER FOUR Unsealing the Past — 45

CHAPTER FIVE Ghosts and Churchyards — 61

CHAPTER SIX Pirates and Thieves — 69

CHAPTER SEVEN White Knight — 79

CHAPTER EIGHT Mad Dogs and Englishmen — 89

CHAPTER NINE Relics and Rum — 99

CHAPTER TEN Charleston, SC — 109

CHAPTER ELEVEN Follow the Trail — 123

CHAPTER TWELVE Moody v. Douglas — 131

CHAPTER THIRTEEN Miracle — 143

CHAPTER FOURTEEN Red, Red Wine — 159

CHAPTER FIFTEEN Sleep Well, Angel — 169

APPENDIX 1 The Island of Barbados — 171

APPENDIX 2 Family Trees	173
BIBLIOGRAPHY	177

CHAPTER ONE
Wrecking Ball

The two men faced off on either side of the net. They leaned forward, concentration etched on their faces and sweaty hands gripping racquets. The sun was pounding down on them, covering them like a hot blanket. But this was no game; it was war.

"This is it," Henry said as he reached up, ready to serve. "Loser pays for drinks." And he slammed the tennis ball across the net like a bomb.

As his buddy Dan lunged for the ball, Henry added, "I see your old house met the wrecking ball." Looking up, Dan nearly missed the ball.

"Which one," he asked, frowning with concern, trying to gather himself and move into a better position. "The Properties or Ambleside, Dundarave?"

Henry met the ball with grace, saying, "Dundarave," as he lobbed another bomb.

"No!" Dan shouted, "Not that historic old house!" as the ball shot by him.

Henry cheered.

"Dammit, Henry," Dan said with disgust. "That was a cheap trick."

"Realtor's privilege." Henry grabbed his towel and began wiping off his sweat, ruffling his normally tidy dark hair.

"Are you being serious, though, about my house?"

"Sadly."

"Jeez, who are these people?" Dan grabbed his towel and wiped his face with vigorous swipes. "It was the original farmhouse in the area when West Van was just one big orchard." He shook his head and picked up a bottle of water. "Nothing's sacred these days to money hungry real estate

1

developers"—he gave Henry a dark look—"and their aiders and abettors at council."

"Hey, man, a guy's gotta make a living. But that wasn't my deal. You know people need a place to live."

"It probably sold for condos or a monster house." He shook his head.

"Hey," Henry said, "I didn't mean to, you know, I just was trying to throw you off your game."

"It's not just that …" Dan shook his head again and picked up his bag.

"Look, I'll buy the drinks." Henry collected his things, slung his bag over his arm, and clapped Dan on the shoulder. They made their way into the bar. The dark, cool pub made a welcoming contrast to the hot summer sunshine.

Sitting in a booth, a cold frothy lager in hand, Henry looked shrewdly at his friend and asked, "So, what's up?"

Dan took a long sip before answering. "I might have cancer."

"Oh, man—"

"It's okay, I'm not dying," he looked down, "yet."

"How bad is it?" Henry asked softly.

"I don't know." It had been a tough week for Dan, thinking about his own mortality. "I have to have my six-month prostate cancer checkup. It's got me worried about it this time." He laughed without humour. "What if this is it? The big C."

"But you … Have you had any tests yet?"

"Too scared to."

Henry leaned forward. "Dan," he said evenly, "this is all in your mind."

Dan shrugged and took another long drink. "I've read all about it. There can be side effects … it can … um"—Henry leaned forward, his face creased with concern—"interfere with your love life."

"Jeez, Dan." Henry sat back in the booth with a thump. "I thought you were dying."

"Well, it concerns me!"

"It concerns all of us. All the stuff we don't know that's lurking out there. You can't take everything to heart. This isn't you," he gestured towards him. "Maybe you're just having a mid-life crisis."

"I guess. This whole business, cancer, my old house, it feels like the last straw."

Henry grabbed Dan's arm. "You're not … thinking about … offing yourself?"

"No, you idiot," Dan replied, shaking off Henry's hand. "I'm thinking of heading to Barbados."

"Barbados?" Henry signalled the server for another round. "That's where you're from, right?"

"Yeah. I don't know. I feel … it's where I was happiest." He shrugged and drained his drink. "I emigrated when I was nineteen. Landed in *la belle province* to go to university in Montreal. Met some French women." He smiled at the server as she placed another beer in front of him. She smiled back.

"Well, I think it's a great idea," Henry said, grabbing back Dan's attention. "Might be just what you need." He picked up his beer. "A toast. To new love and adventure, hurricanes and bikinis." They clinked glasses.

"Amen."

"Have a safe trip, Dan."

"Don't worry about me, Henry. I'll beat this thing."

Henry just shook his head.

When they left the pub and said their good-byes, Dan decided to drive by his old house to see for himself. As he neared his old address, he couldn't believe his eyes. It looked like a disaster, a tangled mountain of old-growth splintered wood and twisted metal, and windows of old wavy glass smashed in their frames, lying amid the heap. Something that had lasted generations, destroyed in a few hours.

He looked past the wreck to the view beyond. The house had sat on the brow of a hill overlooking Vancouver and its port. Up on the top floor, he'd had a 180-degree view: Mt. Baker in Washington State in the east, Vancouver Island in the west, and beautiful Pacific sunsets.

In the old days, there would have been fruit orchards. The house was built in the Southern plantation style, with a pillared entrance and decks overlooking the ocean. In the summer, he used to sleep outside on the deck, under the stars. You could see the freighters lying at anchor in the port, their lights shining into the night.

He had settled in West Vancouver because it reminded him of the little seaside village of Worthing in Barbados where he'd grown up. West Van had the same sounds of waves, smells of seaweed, and ocean sights.

He had been married once. That didn't last. He was a father of two now-grown-up girls; he used to be their hero. He looked at the devastation and knew it wasn't just the house that was lost. But that period of his life was now over. He was single again at fifty.

"It's time to celebrate," he said a little cynically.

Dan got back in his car and turned the key to start the engine. Then, on a whim, keeping it in park, he flipped down the visor to look in the mirror.

He'd always been told he was handsome. He liked the way his brown hair was greying at the edges. He was lean and fit. He didn't have many wrinkles. Some said that he looked a lot younger than his years. He didn't object to that assessment, although sometimes it could get him in trouble. Maybe that's why younger women seemed to be attracted to him. Maybe it was his roguish smile. He smiled sexily into the mirror, and then grimaced.

"You're an idiot," he said aloud.

He slammed up the visor and put the car in drive. He was going to the beach.

***

Ambleside was a long beach of brown sand along the shore of the little seaside village of West Vancouver. Dan swung his car into the parking lot and climbed back out into the hot sun. Down by the water, the cooling west coast wind soothed the unrelenting heat.

He walked onto the sand, threading his way through the masses of kelp, broken shells, and abandoned local Dungeness crab backs. Waves lapped onto the beach and slid back into the ocean.

A few hearty swimmers were daring the frigid waters of the Pacific Ocean. Children were busy on the beach building sandcastles. Portuguese and Asian fishermen were out in the water hauling in their nets. Seagulls and other seabirds hovered overhead, with the occasional bald eagle and blue heron swooping in to celebrate the beautiful day. As he walked farther up the beach, Dan could see the volleyball courts filled with different teams of volleyball players.

He sat on a log and looked out to sea. It was the major shipping channel going into the Port of Vancouver, with a constant flow of little seagoing tugs taking barges up the coast or bringing them into the port. A big cruise ship was out there. It would pass under the Lions Gate Bridge on its way from Alaska. Occasionally, a container ship would blow its horn to get the smaller boats out of its way.

Dan sat there inhaling the fresh salty sea air as memories came flooding back of another beach many thousands of miles away, where, instead of four seasons, it was perpetual summer and the Atlantic Ocean and Caribbean sea was swimmable every day of the year. He had spent most of his first nineteen years on that beach.

I'll probably pay for all that sun exposure, he thought. He couldn't face the prospect of skin cancer either. He looked around for something to cover his arms with and saw a discarded towel. He couldn't see its owner nearby and figured it was abandoned.

He snuggled into the towel as the ocean breezes ruffled his hair, trying not to think about his new worries. His eyes watched the swimmers out in the water and settled on one strong swimmer. She had a natural athletic grace. Her strong strokes cleaved the water. She suddenly stood up in waist-deep water. His mouth went dry. She was beautiful. She grabbed her mass of dark curly hair and smoothed it out of her face. Then she shaded her eyes and looked straight at him.

He wondered if she was Norwegian. For some strange reason, Dan had always been fascinated by Norwegian girls. And he wasn't picky. Blondes, brunettes, it didn't matter. Maybe it was the names that excited him. Names like Tami, Margit, Ingrid, and Sigrid. For most of his life, he'd admired them from afar.

The Norwegian girls he knew in Barbados always seemed to have very, very big brothers with names like Erik, Arvid, and Bjorn, all solidly built with lantern jaws and rippling biceps. Maybe it was those rugged winters, cross country skiing, and rowing the many fjords. For whatever reason, they were much bigger than him, and misbehaving with their sisters could have been damaging to his slender frame. So he'd appraised them from afar.

But this goddess was moving gracefully out of the water till she was standing right before him.

"Dat ees my tah-vel?" she said in a sexy Norwegian accent.

It was love at first sight. All Dan could do was clutch the towel and feel like he was going to swoon. If he passed out in front of her, he'd have to kill himself.

"Dan," he said through dry lips.

"Excuuze me?"

"My name … is Dan. What's yours?"

"Astrid."

Dan pinched himself to see if he was dreaming.

"Please, my tah-vel?" When it suddenly dawned on him, Dan thrust the towel at her.

"You are cute," she said smiling as she began to dry her body.

Dan swallowed as he watched her. She looked like a film star, with long classy legs, deep riveting brown eyes, and a flirtatious twinkle in her eye. He thought she must be about thirty. What was she doing even looking at him?

"Astrid," he said. When he said her name, he thought he'd found his future.

Wow, how lucky can you be at fifty? he thought. *It took me this long in life to fulfill my dream of loving and hopefully marrying a real life beautiful Norwegian.* Marriage would come later, of course; first the courtship and the challenge of convincing her that he was the one for her forever, despite their ages.

"It's hot out here," he said. "Would you like to get a drink?"

Soon he was back in a dark pub, sipping a cold beer, talking about life. She said she liked to swim in the ocean—"I do too!" exclaimed Dan—although she thought the ocean in Vancouver, being the Pacific, was very cold even in midsummer. Dan sipped his beer, imagining them sitting together on the beach after a frigid swim, huddling together for the warmth of their body contact on a beach blanket. It would be a repeat of his teenage Barbados years and he was still up to the excitement of it all. When he got back home he would exclaim loudly, *Thank God for Norway!*

As she chatted in her sexy accent and checked her phone periodically—*these young kids*, he chuckled to himself—Dan was getting the feeling he'd soon be exploring her fjords.

"You drive me home?" she suddenly asked, tucking her phone into her purse and draining her drink, "I walked here."

"Uh, of course." Dan quickly pulled some bills out of his pocket and threw them on the table as she strode ahead through the door like a fashion model.

When they got in the car, he was fumbling with his keys when Astrid suddenly turned to him and showed her athleticism. She grabbed him and soon they were making out like teenagers. At some point in the midst of it, she snapped a selfie.

She sat back, with a cat-caught-the canary, self-satisfied smile and Dan's ego started purring. She couldn't keep her hands off him! Maybe she found a car more exciting than a dull bedroom at home.

Then she sat back with a little pouty expression, said, "That way," and waved her hand to direct him. When they pulled into the parking lot of her four-storey walk-up, she climbed onto him and started putting him through some paces. He couldn't help looking over her shoulder to see if there was any risk of getting caught. After all, it was broad daylight. And to be honest, it was very uncomfortable for a man of his age to be doing any contortions in a small car. Never look a gift horse in the mouth, his mother said, but he thought his leg was getting a cramp. Just as suddenly, she sat back, pulled out her phone, and snapped a selfie. Her lips looked pouty from their make-out session.

"Take me up to my apartment," she ordered, and Dan was excited that after their little lovemaking-appetizer in the parking lot, he'd be spending an active night exploring the mountain beauties of Norway.

Inside the apartment, she tossed her bag onto a chair and casually started removing her clothes down to the bikini she was still wearing underneath. She looked at him, raised her eyebrows, and started unbuttoning his shirt. Frankly, it felt a little clinical.

"Faster," she said. She pulled off his shirt and began undoing his pants, pulling them down over his hips. His excitement was getting pretty apparent. Nothing wrong with his equipment yet. When his pants were down around his ankles, the phone rang. They both froze.

The answering machine kicked in, and an angry, very male Norwegian voice flooded into the room, "Astrid! Vat are you playing at! I am pulling up to your apartment! If he's in there, I'll kill him!"

"Who the hell is that?" Dan asked.

"My ex-husband. He is very jealous type." Dan jerked in fear but stood there frozen. She picked up her bag and began rummaging around in it. "He's a pilot." She drew out a lipstick and began painting dark red on her lips. "You have about ten minutes to get down the elevator before he kills you."

That seemed to unfreeze his mind. A vanishing act was now necessary. Dan pulled up his pants, grabbed his shirt, put it on quickly, and ran to the elevator. He saw a Nordic looking guy getting out of the other elevator. He ran to his car in the alley below the building.

"You sonuvabitch, I kill you!" yelled a very angry man out the window above.

Dan scrambled to his feet, threw himself at his car, hurt his leg, got in, and to the mantra of *"key in the ignition, key in the ignition,"* got the car started and squealed out of the parking lot. He drove madly, heart pounding, glancing back in his rear-view mirror, expecting some maniacal sports car to come zooming up and smash him off the road. When he finally pulled into his own driveway, he dropped his head onto his steering wheel and just stayed there till his breathing returned to normal. Then he pulled down his visor to look into the mirror.

"You're an idiot, Dan the man. Like a failed movie hero. It's time to get out of Dodge."

He limped into his house, threw his keys onto the kitchen counter, went to the fridge, and pulled out a beer. Then he saw the red light flashing on his answering machine. For a moment, he froze again in fear; then he remembered Astrid and her crazy ex didn't have his number. He pushed the button.

"Dan," an excited voice called out, "it's Mary." She was his Aunt Mary in Barbados. "I got something down here that you'll be interested in. Can't say too much over the phone, but it involves a family mystery. I need some help solving it. Call me."

"Guess you better buy a ticket, Dan," he said to himself. "Looks like there's a Barbados adventure waiting for us."

CHAPTER TWO
Ladies' Man

Dan sipped his beer in the little plastic cup and stared out the window at the white fluff of cumulus clouds. The flight from Vancouver to Toronto had been uneventful, and then in Toronto, he had picked up a new seat partner. He was liking this leg of the trip much better.

The blonde to his right stirred in her seat and snuggled into his shoulder. She was the spitting image of one of his teenage girlfriends in Barbados. Her name had been Patricia. It seemed everywhere he looked, he was reminded of Barbados. Dan looked down at the woman. She was beautiful. He enjoyed the warmth of her closeness and let her sleep. She smelled nice; he liked her perfume. He moved his nose from side to side slightly as he breathed in deeply. Maybe Chanel.

She woke with a start and jerked her head off his shoulder. "I'm sorry," she said. "You should have moved me."

"I've been enjoying your company," he joked. "Always happy to provide support to a beautiful woman." Her hair was mussed from sleep and she may have drooled a bit on his shoulder.

She wiped her mouth, put a hand to her hair, and laughed. "Come on now; I must look a mess."

"Do you think I would have let you sleep there if you were a mess?" He gave her his most charm-the-ladies smile.

"What would you have done?"

"I'd have pushed your head off me."

She looked a bit shocked. "That wouldn't have been very nice."

"Well my arm is very special to me."

She narrowed her eyes, assessing him. Then she pursed her lips. "Do you get into a lot of trouble?"

"Well I like some kinds of trouble." His smile turned roguish. "Chanel No. 5, right?"

Her eyes opened in surprise. "Yes."

"I like it." He sniffed the air slightly between them; it seemed to heat up a little. "Maybe you could rest your head on my shoulder a little bit more."

She gave a broad smile. "Sorry to disappoint you, but I'm meeting my boyfriend for a little vacation in Barbados." She tilted her head. "But, maybe I wish I wasn't meeting him, now that I've met you."

He placed his palm on his heart. "I will remember you forever." Then he held out his hand and said, "I'll remember you better if I know your name. My name's Dan."

She took his hand. "I'm Siggy." Dan's eyes widened in surprise. "Well, it's Sigourney," she added, "but my friends all call me Siggy."

"You're … Norwegian?"

Siggy frowned prettily. "You don't like Norwegians?"

"I do, but they usually don't like me." He waved his hand. "It's a long story."

"I'm originally from Norway, but I've been living in BC until recently."

"A BC Norwegian? You don't happen to know any Astrids, do you?"

"Nope. My mother is an Ingrid." She laughed. "Is that good enough?"

A steward came walking down the aisle with a large clear trash bag, picking up their snack leftovers.

Dan drained the last of his beer and handed it to the steward as he said to Siggy, "So you moved recently, you said. Are you living in Toronto?"

"No," she said. "Chatham."

"Chatham."

"That's east of Toronto."

"I used to live in London, Ontario," Dan said, "for university."

"Western?"

"Yeah. Do I look like a Western man?"

"You must be smart. I hear it's tough."

Dan assessed her. "Said like someone who's smarter and buttering someone up. So why are there so many Norwegians in BC?"

"Because of all the fjords, of course. It's like finding a bit of Norway." Siggy tilted her head and asked. "So, business or pleasure?"

Dan blushed.

Siggy laughed. "I mean, are you going to Barbados for business or pleasure?"

"Oh, no, I'm going to check out a family mystery."

"That's intriguing."

The captain's voice came over the intercom and announced they would be starting their descent. They sat their chair backs up and tightened their seatbelts. Dan looked out the window. He felt himself relax under the influence of the bright blue Caribbean sky and the blue sea below. He would soon be home.

Siggy reached under the seat in front of her and pulled out her purse. She rooted around in it and pulled out a compact and a lipstick.

"So, are you meeting up with your boyfriend right away?" Dan asked her, enjoying the sight of her making herself up. "If you have any time, I could show you the sights. I'm from Barbados. You could have your own personal tour guide."

Siggy looked at him, one eyebrow raised. "My boyfriend will be there to pick me up."

"Why didn't you fly together?"

"He was there already on business."

"What's his name?"

Siggy pulled out her phone and showed Dan a picture of a handsome, broad-shouldered man. He was wearing a tank top and flexing his pecs.

"Does Tarzan have a name?"

Siggy chuckled. "Al. And don't let him see you near me. He's the very jealous type."

"Another daughter of Norway with a jealous man," Dan murmured.

"What's that?"

"Norwegian girls seem to have a type."

"And you're not their type?"

"Sadly no."

They sat back in their seats for the final taxi down the runway. As the plane stopped and people started grabbing their bags and streaming towards the exit, Dan took Siggy's hand and lightly kissed it as she watched, surprised and charmed.

"It was really great to meet you, Siggy. I hope you have a great time; it's a lovely place to visit. That's my phone number"—he had slipped his business card into her hand—"just in case you need it." Then he winked. "Say hi to Tarzan."

She laughed, gave him a little nod, and then moved into the aisle. She was soon swallowed up by the stream of people. Dan sat back down to let the crowd thin.

Arrival in Barbados meant the pain in the neck of immigration clearance, baggage collection, and customs clearance. At least he would spend less time in the process than the tourists. As a Barbadian born, he'd go through a much shorter immigration line for locals. The foreign tourists would have to line up, three lanes deep, to get through.

He sped through immigration without a problem, but the baggage took a long time to arrive. A short man in a straw hat was pacing impatiently back and forth in front of Dan. He stopped for a moment and said, "My friend told me she had to wait three days to get her baggage!"

"That right?" Dan answered.

"Yeah, ever since Canada made marijuana legal, they're using sniffer dogs to sniff our luggage." The man was sweating profusely, "They only have one dog."

"That right?" Dan stepped a little away from the man, just to show they weren't together.

He sought the help of a Red Cap, an airport porter wearing a red-billed cap, who pulled his luggage off the conveyor belt and ushered it outside where they were met by his niece, Silvia.

"Uncle Dan!" she cried, rushing to hug him. She looked young and fresh. Her brown hair was tied back and her brown eyes held warmth. "We've missed you!"

"Little Silvi," he replied, returning the hug with a squeeze. "It's been too long. You're not a tiny tot anymore! Are you still in high school?"

She laughed. "I work now in one of the local accounting firms that deal in offshore business."

"A bean counter."

She raised an eyebrow. "We count a lot of beans."

As Dan threw his luggage into the trunk of her dusty blue car, they chatted up a storm, catching up on local news and family gossip. Before he got into the car, he saw Siggy pulling her luggage out through the glass doors. Her hulking boyfriend was standing by his car, a frown on his face.

"You're late," Dan heard him say. *What kind of greeting is that?*

"No, I'm not," Siggy said with a sigh. She reached up to kiss Tarzan, and he nuzzled her ear. Then he obviously and very publicly grabbed her butt.

Dan grimaced. How could she like that kind of treatment?

Then Tarzan deliberately turned his head and looked right at Dan as if daring him.

Boy, Dan thought, *he must be crazy jealous. He doesn't even know I know her.* Shaking his head, he got into his niece's car.

He'd rented an apartment at Abivale near Accra Beach in Rockley. Rockley was the next beach over from Worthing, where he'd grown up. As they drove along the ABC Highway, Dan took a quiet moment to enjoy the regal royal palm trees and grey sago palm trees interspersed along the highway. They maneuvered around a series of roundabouts, before driving through the villages of St. Lawrence, Worthing, and Rockley. Silvia pulled up in front of a bright coral-coloured three-storey apartment surrounded by swaying trees. There were no other buildings nearby.

He gave her a kiss, promised to see her once he was settled, and then lifted his luggage out of the trunk. He waved as the blue car pulled back onto the road and sped off.

He had made sure to choose an apartment facing east so he could sit on the balcony and feel the trade winds blowing across the island from the east. Once inside his apartment, he dropped his bags and went out onto the balcony. All he could see was open sky, breadfruit trees, and a nearby coconut tree blowing in the breeze. He could hear their palm fronds swishing as they moved to and fro, to and fro. He closed his eyes and listened. It was just like being back in his old home, a house called Erindale, which was not far away with almost the same view.

After freshening up and fortifying himself with a cold beer, he threw on a bathing suit and put on a wide-brimmed hat to protect his skin (*you can never be too careful* being his new motto). He went down to Accra beach to inhale the fresh sea air, bask in the brilliant sunshine, and have his first dip in the warm, emerald-green ocean water. It was a sacred moment, stepping into the water. *I'm home*, he thought. That's when he saw her standing majestically by the coral reef in a tiny swimsuit, looking regal, her long hair blowing in the breeze.

She might have been the heroine of a movie. *Wide Sargasso Sea* came to mind—that passionate, sensual book by Jean Rhys. Like Antoinette, Jean's French Creole heroine from Martinique, this goddess in the sea also had long, dark-brown hair that fell over a voluptuous body with small breasts, curving hips, and long legs. She had been a big tease in the movie, with her sultry accent, she teased her newly English arrived husband almost to his despair.

She was like a siren, and Dan found himself wading through the water towards her.

"Are you by any chance Antoinette," he asked her, "the passionate beauty of the *Wide Sargasso Sea*?"

She laughed a trilling laugh and swept her long hair to the side. "Sounds like a mermaid."

"Or a siren," he said smiling. He felt his charm burning bright and moved a bit closer. "My name is Dan Graham." Then her cell phone rang. *Cell phone! Where was she hiding a cell phone in that bikini?*

"Sorry," she said, "gotta go," and she began moving away through the water. But she turned back and grinned, "Maybe I'll see you around." Then, in a flash, she was gone.

"Damn cell phones," he muttered.

Dan always seemed to get along well with the fairer sex, his current luck notwithstanding.

He lay back in the water, totally relaxed. It felt good to be back in his island paradise, back in his old childhood neighbourhood, with the same access to the cooling winds that made the winters in Barbados so delightful. Twenty-two degrees Celsius at night, and twenty-eight during the day.

Accra Beach was a long stretch of lovely white sand. Here on the eastern side, it was sheltered by a coral reef so the water was calm and sheltered. It was good for families and children, with deckchairs and beach umbrellas. On the western side, there was no reef, only open sea with big waves and a heavy surf, with five-foot waves crashing in.

When he'd had enough of floating, Dan got out of the water. He decided to make his way to Worthing Beach, east of Accra. He walked up the beach, past the crowds of tourists speaking Quebecois French, across the road, and through the little lane that led from Accra to Worthing.

He had turned his head to watch an array of micro-swimsuits when he saw the statuesque beauty from the coral reef again, his Antoinette. He took a couple steps in her direction when a voice called out in Bajan accent, "Is that Dan Graham, the ladies' man from Worthing Beach!"

Dan looked towards the voice and saw a slightly paunchy, well-tanned Caucasian man. He was slightly balding on top and obviously knew him. He was wearing colourful shorts, a clashing shirt, and Dan could smell Brylcreem from where he stood. All the Bajan boys used to put Brylcreem in their hair. Dan squinted his eyes a bit and looked hard at him.

"Tommy?"

"In the flesh."

"Tommy the terrible?"

Tommy threw back his head and laughed. "Damn right, Tommy the terrible teen, although I'm a bit older now. Seeing you brings back all those wonderful years spent on these beaches chasing girls, catching fish, and digging for shells; though, the shells are nearly all gone now as the tourists pick it clean. You back from the Arctic?"

"Yeah, I'm back for a visit from cold Canada." Then he nodded towards his Antoinette. "D'you know who that beauty is over there?"

"No clue, but she sure is cute and curvaceous. How are you, man? Where's that wife I heard you have? They say you gave up roving around and settled down." He looked towards Antoinette and raised his eyebrow. "Or so they say."

"I did," Dan said, "but after raising a couple kids, she had enough of me and wanted to go her own way." He shrugged. "I'm back to a being a bachelor."

"I better warn the local girls that the king of charm is back in town." Tommy gave a wolf howl, and heads up and down the beach turned in their direction. "Welcome home. We still have the fish to fish and the girls to chase."

"So what do you do these days for a living to get enough money to chase the women?"

"I run a tour company, and I still run along this beach with my throwing net. I still catch those little sprats, and occasionally," he said out of the corner of his mouth, "I catch a tourist or two." He looked out over the beach and smacked his lips.

"So I take it no permanent relationship?"

"Like you, I had one. But she left me for a richer guy." His machismo seemed to deflate. "Too bad; she was pretty nice. You remember Arlene? The redhead from Worthing Beach?"

"Oh yeah, I remember her. She was one great piece of architecture, the only redhead in the neighbourhood"—Tommy frowned at Dan's words—"and really smart too, as I recall." Seeing Tommy's look, Dan changed the subject. "Sure you don't know that beauty over there?"

"Wish I did. She's new to the beach."

"I hear the beach has been invaded by the Sargassum seaweed."

"Yeah," Tommy said. He looked kind of glum. "Everything's changing, man." Then he stood tall, as if putting aside old memories. "Well, I gotta go. Let's get together and talk about old times." He punched Dan lightly on the arm.

"Sure, that would be fun."

Dan decided to make his way back to his apartment and call his Aunt Mary to find out what this family mystery was all about. On his way back down the beach, a big cloud suddenly moved in, and it started to rain in one of those tropical showers that seem to suddenly break the sky open.

As he jogged along the beach back to Accra, he tripped over something. It was a beautiful butterfly-shaped Tellin shell; the locals called them Aurora shells. It was yellow and white, the sides of the shell looking like the wings of a butterfly.

It was unusual to find an Aurora on this beach as the sea pool where the Tellins lived was on the far eastern end of the beach at Worthing. Maybe another sign of climate change moving things around. He picked up and tucked it safely in his pocket. As the rain turned into a heavy deluge, Dan ducked under the closest beach umbrella.

"I'm so sorry," he said as crouched under the umbrella, wiping rain out of his eyes, "do you mind if I just—"

"Dan!"

He looked up. "Siggy?" It was Siggy from the flight, looking luscious in a tiny bikini and wide-brimmed hat.

"Of all the umbrellas in all the world, I walked into yours," he said out of the corner of his mouth. "Where's Tarzan gone off to?"

She laughed. "Don't be so jealous. My man is in the sea. To keep his muscles, he must swim back and forth, and back and forth. Too boring for me."

"I'd think he'd just go into the jungle and climb some trees. There are lots of monkeys in Barbados. He would feel right at home."

Siggy touched his arm. "Dan, you're bad."

"Where are you staying?" Dan asked.

"Accra Resort."

"I'm just across the road! How lucky can a guy get?"

Before she could answer, a wet angry face popped under the umbrella. "Who the hell are you!" Dan took a step back to the edge of the umbrella. Tarzan stepped under the umbrella, bending because of his height and said, "You better leave my woman alone or I'll smash your pretty face!"

"Thanks for the compliment, but I'm really more into women." With that Dan waved to Siggy and ran out into the rain, daring a glance back to see if Tarzan was bearing down on him. He could see Siggy hanging onto him. *Thank you, Siggy.*

He walked off the sand onto grass, through the stands of evergreen casuarina trees and coconut palms, through the taxi lot, and crossed the busy road, being careful not to get "licked down," as the locals would say when hit by a passing car.

He made it safely home, and after a shower went to the Chefette restaurant chain next door, the local edition of McDonald's, for a dinner of soup and salad. When he got back to his apartment, he poured himself some rum, put on some Bob Marley reggae, *No Woman No Cry* and went to sit outside on his balcony.

The moon was bright—Dan could see the whole sky lit up. He listened to the sound of the waves on the beach across the road and the swaying of the palm trees and felt happy.

He punched his aunt's number on his cell phone.

"Hi Mary."

"Are you home?"

"Yeah," he paused and looking out to the night, "I'm home."

"I'll come pick you up first thing tomorrow."

"The waves sound different here than in Vancouver," he said. Dan could also hear little whistling frogs singing in a chorus. They would come out at night to serenade Barbados.

"Listen, Dan, I want you to come to the Yacht club tomorrow and meet my friend John."

"Is he a *special* friend?"

"No, you idiot, he's a local historian. Big in the local research community. Does it in his spare time."

Dan chuckled and took a sip of rum. It went down smoothly. "Are you still playing the piano?"

"In my spare time." Dan thought he could hear her smiling into the phone.

"Well, don't party too much tonight."

"Dan, I'm considered a senior now. I'm getting too old for parties." Now they both chuckled. "Okay, I'm not partying as much." Mary loved going to parties.

"Can you give me a clue?" Dan asked.

"Better wait till tomorrow. I want to get my facts straight."

"Well, Mary, I'm all ears and looking forward to learning more tomorrow."

"Dan," she said seriously as they wrapped up the phone call, "I'm glad you're home."

"Me too," he replied as he looked out at the horizon, the moonlight lighting up the water. "Me too."

Dan then called his sister Jessica to let her know that he had arrived and that he was meeting with Aunt Mary tomorrow at the Yacht club. They would get together later.

Ladies' Man

***

Mary pulled up to the front door of his apartment in her little black car, leaned out the window, and waved. She looked as beautiful as ever with her bouffant brown hair, shimmering silver highlights, and Irishy-white skin complexion.

"You look great," Dan said as he folded himself up into the passenger seat.

"Long time no see, Dan," she said smiling.

"There's no way you can be almost sixty." He shook his head in amazement.

"You got to stay active when you're old like me. I swim every day at the Yacht club in the ocean." She stepped on the gas.

Dan enjoyed the lovely breeze through his open window; he watched the swaying palms. As they arrived at the Yacht club, without slowing, Mary swung the car into the opening in the coral walls, pulled around a circular driveway, and passed by a little security house and the tennis courts. She then turned left into a little gap and parked abruptly close to the beach.

They got out, and Mary led him through a little green gate into the beachside bar and kitchen, where green wooden tables were spread out on the sand under the very low-lying seagrape and mahoe trees that shaded the tables like umbrellas.

"This place hasn't changed at all since I was a teenager," Dan said, looking around. "Remember the Old Year's Night party?"

"You were so proud of your tux. You danced in it all night."

"Then I had to get up early to sail in the New Year's Day regatta in my International 14." He smiled wistfully. "I miss those days."

"You're feeling nostalgic because this place hasn't changed a bit."

The Royal Barbados Yacht Club, as it used to be called, was a true representative of the old colonial system. . You had to be voted in to become a member, and even one little black ball could prevent you from joining. Sitting under the trees on the beach were many old English colonials who had never left Barbados, and mainly local Whites. There were also English visitors and other tourists who bought a shorter membership for their stay.

Aunt Mary was a member, as had been Dan's father; he used to invite them there for a beachside drink. He had passed away when Dan was twenty-five—his mother, ten years ago.

"Do they still serve those terrific rum punches, and the Bentleys," Dan said excitedly, "with the lemonade and cherry?"

"Yes, Dan," she laughed, "and I'll order a fish cake appetizer with their spicy sauce."

As they sat drinking rum punch and munching fish cakes, Dan sighed with pleasure. "These are the best fish cakes I've ever eaten. I wish I could get the recipe."

"You cook now?"

"I have some talents, you know. In Canada I like making pakoras. They're like a spicy Indian fritter. Goes great with beer."

"Good for you. I'm impressed. Most of the Barbadian men I know stay as far away from the kitchen as they can."

"Well, when you go to a new country on your own, you learn to cook or die of starvation."

The Yacht club was a popular spot. Once the home of the commander of the Royal Engineers during colonial days, the old mansion now housed a main dining room, a bar, dressing rooms and showers, a ballroom, and a trophy room, its walls lined with photographs. A photo of his father's B class boat was on that wall, as Dan would proudly tell his friends in his youth. In the front and back of the club were the tennis courts. There was also a boatyard, where the members stored their boats, and an outside shower for swimmers and sunbathers. There was even a bowl to wash off the sand when you came out of the sea.

Recently the beach and sea had been invaded by the Sargassum seaweed, which appalled the old-time members, who had never seen that before. Their little time capsule was supposed to be sacrosanct from such invasions. No doubt more evidence of climate change.

As they finished up their fish cakes, the little green gate opened and a very tall Black man with horn-rimmed glasses stepped through.

As he came over to their table, Dan could smell his aftershave lotion.

"Welcome to Barbados," the man said solemnly by way of greeting.

"Dan, this is John the historian, he is a graduate of the University of the West Indies" Mary said.

"Hi, John," Dan said with a wave.

"I trust your trip was a pleasant one?" John asked still standing by the table.

"Long, but worth taking to get to this paradise," Dan said with a sweep of his hand.

"John, please sit down," Mary said gesturing to a chair.

"Yes, have a rum punch," Dan said, lifting his glass. "They are the best."

"I think I will sit," John said, pulling out a chair. "My bones and joints are a bit creakier than they used to be."

Dan looked at Mary and raised his eyebrows. The man sounded kind of pompous.

Mary flashed her eyes at Dan. "John, here, is very well educated and very knowledgeable about all things historical."

"Thank you very much," John said very formally. "I suppose you'd like me to 'cut to the chase,' as they say," he said jauntily—Dan would have laughed, but Mary was looking daggers at him—"and talk about your family before the rum punch dulls my memory."

"My family?" Dan asked with a start.

"Well, boy, your family is one of the oldest in the island"—Dan frowned at the word "boy" but did not interrupt him—"having come a year after the first settlement by the English in 1627. Yours came in 1628 and was on the list of settlers owning more than ten acres of land in 1628. That was long before the days of Black slavery, but they did use indentured White servants. Your family were the ten-acre men, who farmed their farms, not plantations, with their own family. They were originally from Devon, of Norman heritage, and went over to England with William the Conqueror in 1066.

"Later, other related members of the family, English aristocrats also from Devon, came to Barbados. They were part of the English Royalist gentry, who were finally defeated at the Battle of Naseby in 1645, by Oliver Cromwell." He looked at their empty plates on the table. "I wouldn't mind a plate of those delicious-looking fish cakes." Mary jumped up and went to order more drinks and fish cakes.

"The English Royalists fled to Barbados in droves once they lost their estates in England to Cromwell. These were the ones who brought Black slavery to Barbados. The gentry had never done a stroke of manual labour in their lives, and they found that White political prisoners who were indentured couldn't work in the hot sun planting and cultivating sugarcane. They turned to darker skinned people who were accustomed to working in the hot sun, and who were a cheap source of labour and that was how Black slavery began in Barbados."

"Well, I think," Dan said, "it was more complex than that—" but Mary shook her head slightly. He frowned but changed the topic. "So how does this relate to the mystery Mary mentioned?"

"I will be getting to that," John said dismissively. "The Normans or Norsemen were of course Vikings from Scandinavia—"

"We're Vikings?" Dan said in surprise, looking at his aunt as she came back with rum punch.

She laughed. "It explains a lot."

"Thank you." John took a long sip of rum and smacked his lips. Then he gestured to Dan's hair. "That explains why you were blonde and blue eyed as a child."

Dan frowned again and Mary put a hand on his arm. "I just told him a bit of our own history," she said lightly.

"It was people of mainly Norman ancestry from England who settled the early colonies of Barbados and Virginia, you know." John took another large sip of rum. "Their Viking ancestry never let them sit still for five minutes; they were always off to find somewhere new to conquer."

"Your first ancestor in Barbados settled on the south coast in the parish of Christ Church and built Devon Farm."

Mary jumped up again as the fish cakes were ready and quickly brought them back so as not to miss anything.

"Aw, thank you," John said in appreciation as she set the fish cakes before him. "You are the twelfth generation born in Barbados, from a family that ended up owning a small fifty-acre farm by the time of the emancipation of the slaves in 1838. That farm, Devon Farm, no longer exists, as it's been cut up into various housing developments and lots, and also a cricket ground. You also have a direct ancestor who left agriculture and became a principal or headmaster at a parochial boys' school."

"Our family owned slaves?" Dan asked.

"Your extended family," John clarified around a mouthful of food. "Your immediate family were minor slave owners, with only five slaves."

"But," Dan said, "they still had slaves."

"Your dad always said our family were small farmers," Mary added.

"And farmers they remained," John said, nodding. "They were never part of the plantocracy, otherwise you would have been born in Australia or New Zealand where the rich Grahams went."

"This is very interesting," Dan said, "but before the rum takes over will we get to the mystery?"

"Be patient," John said, once more irritating Dan.

"*Your* mystery," he continued, "starts with your extended family owning a grand plantation called Coral Castle, about 300 hundred acres in the parish of St. John. It was at this location that your mystery occurred—"

Mary broke in excitedly. "It has to do with the disappearance of a small, ten-year-old boy, who was the heir to the plantation—"

"This was in the early eighteenth century, 1710 or thereabouts," John continued, looking slightly miffed at the interruption. "They say he died in a fire; that was very common with children in the days of candles before electricity."

"And he burned to death!" Mary said with a sad look. "Poor little guy."

Dan sighed. "Too bad for the little guy."

"To make matters even more mysterious," Mary added, "the little boy's parents also died in strange circumstances a short time before him—"

"That's when," John interrupted, "the sugar plantation, Coral Castle, passed into the hands of their lawyer, who had letters of administration in the absence of a will of the son."

"However," Mary said, "for years after, local villagers and others have seen a small boy's ghost walking on the grounds of the plantation down by the windmill."

"Wow," Dan said. "That's quite a story."

"I agree," said Mary. "It's exciting." She sat forward, smiling at John to continue.

"To make the mystery even more mysterious," he said, "your direct ancestor from Devon Farm, who was the cousin of the little boy, and executor of the will of the boy's father, and probably your great-great-great-great-great-great-grandfather, died in mysterious circumstances himself. He fell from a horse and broke his neck. Supposedly a snake crossed the road from one cane field to another, causing his horse to rear up and throw him. But that seems odd, as Barbados had imported mongooses from India to kill the snakes, and there were no snakes left in the cane fields of Barbados."

Mary burst out, "It sure looks to me that a whole lot of shenanigans went on in Barbados in those days, and a lot of people got cheated out of what was rightfully theirs."

"Well," John said, finishing up his fish cakes and draining the last of his rum punch, "it sounds like there were some strange and crooked things going on in old Barbados."

"It's certainly worth looking into," Dan said, sitting back in his chair. "I'll need to look at old records."

"I would suggest," John said, wiping his hands fastidiously on a napkin, "going to the Archives to check out family records and then visiting Christ Church churchyard. And as luck would have it, Coral Castle is now up for sale. It might be open for viewing." He pushed back his chair and stood. "And now, I must attend another appointment." He took Mary's hand and clasped it warmly. "Thank you for lunch."

"Thanks for your help, John," she replied.. "We'll be in touch if we run into any obstacles."

As Dan watched the man go back through the little green gate, he murmured, "I was all ready to insist on paying for his lunch, but apparently that wasn't an issue."

Mary laughed and hit him lightly in the arm. "Dan."

"Mary, let's have a swim before it gets too hot."

They went to change into swimsuits and made their way towards the warm, emerald-green sea. The Yacht club had a little pool roped off in the sea, and the water was remarkably free of Sargassum seaweed—so far.

As they floated in the buoyant water, Dan thought about the dead little boy. His childhood was so different from Dan's. He must have felt alone.

Dan looked at the Aquatic club on shore. It was a low, wide structure built on stilts over the water. He used to sit on the verandah as a boy himself and would watch his father sail. He wondered if the little boy had ever had that chance.

A woman was leaning against the railing, looking out at the water. She was long and leggy and looked familiar.

"Dan," Mary said, breaking into his thoughts, "is that lady on the deck up there your old teenage girlfriend, Patricia?"

"Yes, she does look a lot like Patricia." He squinted his eyes. "It's Siggy!"

"Who's that?"

"Siggy. I sat next to her on the plane." He wiggled his eyebrows. "We got along very well."

"Shall I wave to her, then?" She started to lift her hand, but Dan grabbed it.

"No!" He looked around carefully. "Her boyfriend, Tarzan, is probably lurking around close by."

"Tarzan? Is that his real name?"

"Should be."

Mary splashed him and took off swimming. Dan followed her and they swam around the yacht club pool for a bit.

"So what do you think our next move should be?" Mary asked Dan. "John gave us a lot to mull over. Although I am the family historian, your sister Jessica will be taking over from me on this research project, as she is younger and has more energy than me. She was busy today but I will bring her up to speed on our discussions. John, of course, will help."

"I think I need to verify certain facts. We should go to the Archives and the Barbados Museum and Historical Society Library."

"And visit the churchyards and plantations. It's been years since I've done that and never really thought about them being ours."

Dan lay his head back in the water and closed his eyes against the sun. "Visiting Coral Castle would be key since Devon Farm's been razed. I also want to check out the burial records for the Devon Farm farm."

"Well," Mary said, as they started swimming towards the beach, "your research will have to wait a day. Cousin Alison has just arrived from

England with her husband, Ben. You're invited for lunch at the Carriage House in the old Crane Hotel."

"You said 'you.' Aren't you coming with me?"

"As much as I love family," she answered, "I really don't have the time to drive all the way into the country to have lunch, the Crane is so far way"

"Coward," he chastised.

"Yes."

Then he was back to the mystery. "Maybe after lunch I'll visit Coral Castle," he said. "I still can't get over the fact that we owned slaves." He had never considered his Black friends at school anything but Barbadians like him, except a different colour. He hadn't even thought about slavery as local history wasn't taught in the Barbadian schools. It made him unhappy to think his friends' ancestors had been enslaved by White people. He doubted his father's generation would have known about their family's slave-ownership past either. No internet then to search family history, only family Bibles, and Dan recalled their Bible only went back to 1890. He had learned that one of his closest Black friends had in fact become the Headmaster of the school that they had gone to, but his other Black friends had all emigrated to America.

He remembered how, as a student in Montreal, he had once seen an American slavery movie on TV and then, on a Barbados vacation, had talked to a hundred-year-old Barbadian from a planter family.

"Look, man," the old man said, "slavery was a terrible thing. But at the time Barbados was settled, it was legal, an accepted thing, accepted by the Anglican Church, who were slave owners themselves, and even the English aristocracy were slave owners in Barbados."

Dan had voiced his skepticism and responded, "I don't buy it. The planters stole their freedom. Would you like to be owned by someone and have no freedom?"

"Look," the old man continued, "the English were the first to abolish slavery in 1807 and set up the West Africa Squadron of the Royal Navy in 1808 to patrol the coast of West Africa and suppress the slave trade, and freed a lot of slaves, and settled them in Liberia. Did you know that some black Bajans settled in Liberia after Emancipation, and one of their early Presidents, Arthur Barclay, was a Bajan born man? The Brits were the first to free slaves in 1838, compared to Cuba in 1886, and Brazil the last in 1888. It took a civil war in the USA to free their slaves in 1863. The English deserve some credit for that. Equiano, the Black Abolitionist talks in his autobiography, in 1789, about starting as a slave in Barbados and how there was better treatment of slaves here in Barbados."

"There cannot ever be any moral justification for slavery. If I were enslaved in chains," Dan had countered, "I'd be like Bussa, the slave who started the 1816 revolt in Barbados. I'd break my chains and run as fast as I could and head for the seacoast. Then I'd swim as fast as I could and take my chances with the sharks, and who knows, maybe like Equiano, the Black Abolitionist, I'd end up as a bigshot lawyer in England. However I do agree that the British took steps to fix this abomination first, whether it was for economic, or humanitarian reasons doesn't matter, the fact remains that they fixed it before any other slaving nation, even America, and tried to stop others from continuing it."

"Tell yuh one thing I don't agree with," the old man said. "At Emancipation, the English paid all the money to the slave owners and not one red cent to the slave families. Surely to God they could have put aside ten percent of the emancipation monies for the slave families, to give them a little start in life. It was very short-sighted because the Blacks would have become consumers which would have been good for the economy..

"The other real stupid thing the English did," he said, clearly warming to the subject, "was not insisting the slave owners had to stay in Barbados to get their emancipation payouts. They let eighty percent of the planters take their money and run to Australia, New Zealand, America, England, and even Canada. Barbados never recovered and nearly all the plantations went bankrupt. The old man was long dead now, but he would have been pleased to know that they were now talking reparations from the UK for slavery in Barbados.

"I am one hundred percent behind it, of course. It is long overdue and should have been part of a Golden Handshake when Barbados went independent," Dan had said to John earlier.

The old man's words had struck Dan then and they still stuck with him, especially now as he was thinking about his past. And only recently, Dan learned, in 2015 to be exact, have the loans, taken out in 1838 to pay the slave owners, been paid off. Two hundred years later!"

To Dan it now seemed that the descendants of Caribbean slaves who had emigrated to Britain over the years up to 2015 had in fact, through British taxation, subsidised the payments made to the owners of their ancestors way back at Emancipation. A chilling thought.

Dan had asked the historian John why, when Barbados went independent on November 30, 1966, the issue of slavery reparations was never brought up in the negotiations.

He had just shrugged and replied, "I guess no one thought of it."

CHAPTER THREE
Mysteries

Dan found himself in yet another car speeding down a highway. This time, in a practical, grey-coloured car that smelled like a new rental. His cousin Alison was sitting in the front, chatting up a storm and commenting on the beauty of the countryside. Since she didn't seem to require any response, Dan tuned her out and enjoyed the view as they drove past the Graeme Hall Nature Sanctuary, through the countryside of the parish of Christ Church on the Errol Barrow Highway, and then turned onto Highway 6. They drove past the airport road with its royal palms, sago palms, and bougainvillea hedges of pink, orange, red, and purple, and some strange white flowers Dan had never seen before. They passed sugar plantations and villages of little wooden houses and concrete homes and the famous Anglican church of St. Martins.

This part of Barbados, close to the seacoast, was parched and dry compared to the usual lusciousness of the island. Along this coast in the old days, the crop would be cotton rather than sugar, because it needed less rain.

Though now part of a luxury resort, the old Crane Hotel was built in 1887. It was the oldest hotel in the Caribbean and rested on a big cliff overlooking the ocean. Off in the water was the most renowned coral reef in Barbados, the Bow Bells Reef. The beach below it was one of the most beautiful beaches on the island, but the water was quite rough with surf and only good swimmers could handle it. The beach was accessible by an elevator at the top of the cliff and was now filled with deck chairs full of tourists.

The Carriage House where they were going to have lunch had once been a stable for the Crane Hotel. Back in the day, it was visited by local sugar planters and the local White elite, who would go there to soak up the sea air before tourism really came to Barbados. The Carriage House was now a poolside restaurant open on all sides to provide a magnificent view of the sea.

Alison, an attractive brown-haired, blue-eyed Barbadian, who now lived in Northern England with her English husband, was about Dan's age. She led them into the restaurant with the confidence of a woman used to getting her way.

Ben was from Northern England and held strong opinions about all things. When he spoke, Dan detected a whiff of a Yorkshire accent.

After they were seated, Dan searched around for a topic and asked his cousin about Brexit. "What do you think, Alison, is the UK ever going to Brexit or just keep negotiating *ad infinitum*?"

Alison opened her mouth to answer, but Ben cut in. "Since we joined the EU, we've been overrun by Eastern Europeans and other immigrants. They're filling up our medical systems, charging lower rates than English tradesmen, stealing jobs from real Englishmen, and now we're strangers in our own country."

Dan raised his eyebrows. He'd really just been making conversation.

Ben seemed angry and the server who had been approaching the table stopped and then made an about-face back to the kitchen.

Alison cautioned, "Uh, Ben—"

"We have to do something before it's too late and we become like France, Belgium, and Germany, overrun by immigrants and Muslims with Sharia law—"

"Honey," Alison said in a soothing voice, "isn't this the greatest view?"

"—under the EU system we have no control of our borders."

"Surely there must be some benefits that outweigh the negatives," Dan said. He didn't mean to egg Ben on but the man certainly was opinionated. "How about all the agricultural subsidies your farmers get? And the fishing subsidies your fishermen get? Can you afford to lose them?"

"We got along without them before. Losing our country to foreigners is more important than subsidies."

Mysteries

At this point the waiter sidled over again and Alison waved.

"Okay now, everyone. Let's have a wonderful lunch, shall we?" She oohed and ahhed over the menu. Dan ordered the flying fish cutters, which were tasty fish sandwiches, a Caesar salad, and a glass of rum. Ben went for chicken wings and a Carib beer; Alison, a garden salad and a coffee.

The server, a young Barbadian wearing a blue top and black pants, was soon back with their orders. When he placed Dan's rum on the table, he said, "Your glass of Mount Gay."

"What's that?" Ben asked.

"Barbados Mount Gay rum," Dan said. "Named after an ancient Barbados family originally from Bath in England."

This is the oldest rum brand name in existence." Dan took a sip and let the flavour roll on his tongue. To change the subject, he asked, "So, Ben, do you know why the Bow Bells reef is famous?"

"Oh yes," Alison said, perking up at the change of topic, "that's a great story."

"Let's hear it," Ben said. "I'm all ears."

"Sam Lord was one of the most famous buccaneers on the island of Barbados. This was around the turn of the eighteenth century," Dan said.

"He lived in Sam Lord's Castle," Alison said excitedly. "It used to be a plantation house and tourist attraction with incredible antiques, and a truly magnificent parapet roof of fortress-like openings."

"Used to be?" Dan asked.

"Didn't you hear? It was destroyed in a fire sometime since you left Barbados. In 2010, I think."

"That's too bad." He took another sip of rum as Ben shook his head and drank some beer in commiseration. Dan continued "It was a hotel called Sam Lord's Castle when I was a kid. It was a mansion that looked like a castle. It had a lovely open-air dance floor where you could dance under the stars and moonlight, which we did as teenagers, very romantic. When Sam lived there he plundered ships stranded on the reef."

"Legend has it," Alison said, leaning forward, "Sam Lord would hang lanterns in the coconut trees from the beach in front of his house, and trick ships into thinking that it was the port of Bridgetown, the capital city. They would drive their ship ashore and onto the reef and wreck them."

Dan picked up the story. "Sam Lord would then send out his fleet of boats, manned by his slaves, who'd pillage the boats of all they could. They'd bring the loot back to shore and store it in dungeons under the castle.

"One day he supposedly made the mistake of wrecking a ship of the Royal Navy, and that was the end of him. He was taken to England and thrown into a debtors' prison and never came back to Barbados."

"Currently, the Barbados government has plans to rebuild it with Chinese labour and financial help from China," Alison said and then looked quickly at her husband. "But, Dan, we haven't heard about what you've been up to," she added.

They spent the rest of the time pleasantly catching up on what they'd been doing in recent years and enjoying the water view, Dan and Alison making sure to steer the conversation away from anything smacking of politics.

When they were done, and Dan had paid the tab—"I insist," he'd said. "This *is* your vacation as well"—he suggested Alison and Ben take some time to walk around the area, and he would stay and enjoy a bit more of the bar.

"And a bit more quiet, I think," Alison said laughing. "After all, it is *your* vacation as well." She kissed his cheek. "I would love to walk around a bit and recall my childhood in Barbados. We'll meet you back here. Come on, Ben."

Dan decided to chase the rum with some Carib beer and approached the bar. A large, sweaty body stepped in front of him.

The man blocking his way was very drunk and very loud. Short and chubby, he looked fifty-something, with black hair, a greying goatee, and a broad Scottish accent. He seemed to be chatting with anyone who would listen.

Dan tried to get around him when the man said, "Hi there, laddie," in a very drunken voice. The man squinted at him. "Who the hell are you?" Then he clapped Dan on the back. "Tell me yer story."

Laughing, Dan replied, "Well, I'm a Bajan-born laddie, here on the island from cold Canada."

"And what're ye doin' in Barbados?"

Mysteries

"Checking out some family history. You look like you're having a good time. Enjoying the local beer or the rum?"

The man winked. "The rum." He swayed a bit. "So yer a bonny Bajan historian, what? Do I have some history to tell yeh about." Then he bowed, almost falling over. "Yeh have just had the pleasure of meeting Angus Montagu, university history professor in Durham, Northern England."

Dan considered him a moment then shook his hand and said, "Dan Graham."

"Graham, did you say?" Angus said sharply, looking at him as he swayed.

"Yes," Dan smiled, "Graham. Let me buy you a beer."

"Tell you what," Angus said, "why don't we grab that empty table over there and talk in private." Then he leaned in and whispered, "Are you into mysteries?"—Dan nodded—"I have a great one for you." Then Angus winked at him and stumbled towards the empty table.

When Dan came back to the table, Angus was settled in his chair.

The Scot thanked him for the beer and made a toast. "To family histories!"

"To family histories." Dan raised his glass.

"I had an ancestor called Hugh," Angus said. "The bonny lad was an officer and a gentleman, who fought for the Scots at the Battle of Dunbar in 1650. He fought against that devil limey Englishman, Oliver Cromwell, and as the Scots lost the battle, he was imprisoned in Durham Cathedral by Cromwell after the battle." He took a long drink of his beer and then went on. "He was shipped along with 3,000 prisoners to the Caribbean and Barbados to serve seven years as an indentured servant, cutting sugar-cane in the hot sun on a sugar plantation called Coral Gables."

Dan jerked his head. *Did he mean Coral Castle?* "That's interesting," he said.

"He would have been called a 'redleg', Angus continued, "because his pale Celtic skin got burned in the hot sun. That what they called White indentured slaves from Scotland, Ireland, and West England, ye know."

"Lucky for him, he was eventually conscripted into the Barbados militia and sent to St. Kitts by a bigshot Barbados baronet, Sir Timothy Something-something," he waved his hand drunkenly. "Of course, being a good, strong Scot he defeated the Frenchies and conquered St. Kitts." He looked at Dan and frowned menacingly. "Are you following me, laddie?"

Dan nodded. This must be how he treated his students.

"But," Angus whispered, leaning in and raising his finger, "he stole some treasure." He looked over his shoulder around the room. "Have you ever heard of the St. Cuthbert Treasures?" Dan shook his head. "As an officer, he was allowed to carry a tote bag for personal effects. He stashed the wee religious artifacts in this bag and brought it to Coral Gables."

Dan's eyes widened. Angus nodded his head. He leaned forward and looked at Dan with fire in his eyes. "I want to track down the lad's Montagu descendants and find the lost treasure. I want to use it to reward the descendants of those poor Scottish bastards who were shipped to work in the hot Caribbean sugar fields to die from ill treatment and the climate." He sat back and looked up, as if imagining the treasure. "It must be worth something big now as nearly 400 years have passed since the Battle of Dunbar."

"So what you are telling me is that the Scot Montagu stole some of the St. Cuthbert Treasures when he was imprisoned in Durham Cathedral, and was able to bring them with him to Barbados to Coral Gables plantation," Dan asked.

"You got it, laddie." Angus replied.

"How do you know the treasure hasn't been found yet?" Dan asked.

Angus looked around again then leaned in and said in a low voice. "It's a story that's been passed through our family from generation to generation. A cousin who lived in Guyana, where a lot of Scots settled as planters, had met Hugh in Barbados; he got the story from him and passed it on to the family on one of his trips back to Scotland. I've heard tell that the treasure was stolen from Hugh, and then," he furrowed his brow mournfully, "he just disappeared."

"Disappeared?" Dan had a funny feeling about this.

"Poof," Angus said gesturing with his fingers.

"Looks to me like a whole lot of shenanigans went on in Barbados in those days," Dan murmured.

"Of course," Angus continued, "the Durham Cathedral authorities won't admit that anything was stolen from the Cathedral, if there ever was even an inventory of all the stuff. But I'd bet they'd pay a huge reward if it was returned."

Mysteries

Dan tipped his glass to down the rest of his beer. He saw Alison and Ben coming into the restaurant across the room. Alison looked around, saw him at the table, and gave a little wave. "Well, Angus, that's a fascinating story," Dan said, "but I have some people waiting for me."

"It's too bad you didn't have a chance to tell me yer family story, Dan of the Grahams," Angus said.

Dan stood up and reached out to shake his hand. "I wish you the best of luck."

"Cheers, and a wee bit of luck to you and your bonny friends," Angus said. He added in a whisper, "Don't tell my wife, Lynette, about my drinking." He shook his head. "She's not Scottish but Singaporean and doesn't like me drinking. And remember"—he winked—"what I told you is our little secret."

"Sure, just between you and me."

Dan joined his cousin and her husband. As Alison chatted amiably about their stroll around the area, Dan mulled over Angus's story. Could Hugh's plantation be Coral Castle? Was this coincidence? He was visiting Coral Castle today to solve his own family mystery only to find another connected mystery. Could Coral Castle have treasure hidden there, some of the relics of the St. Cuthbert Treasures? Could it have been the cause of all the shenanigans, the crooked lawyer, the death of the little boy, and the other strange family deaths?

Leaving the Crane, they made their way north past St. Philip Parish and St. George Parish and then into St. John Parish. Once they were past Mt. Tabor Moravian Church, which was built in 1825, they went west towards Coral Castle.

The last part of the road was rough, with giant potholes and twists and turns as they rode up to a higher elevation. When they finally saw the house, Alison gasped.

The house was made of coral stone, blackened with age, with vegetable creepers, excess vegetation, and a yard slippery with moss, and there was a *for sale* sign outside of it.

"It's for sale!" Alison exclaimed. "Oh, Ben," she grabbed his arm, "we should buy it! Wouldn't that be great, Dan? Having it back in our family?"

Ben sniffed, looking around the plot of land. It was green and lush and absolutely overrun with vegetation from years of lack of care. There was even a family of local Barbadian green monkeys running around and screeching at their presence. They had cute black faces, black fingers and toes, greenish-grey coats, and long tails. These monkeys had originally come over on the slave ships from Africa. They had stayed and prospered and were now a national hazard, stealing fruits, vegetables, and valuable crops, and scaring horses and other animals. There was a bounty on monkey tails, but they were protected in the nature reserves like the Barbados Wildlife Reserve.

Coral Castle looked imposing but run down.

"It's a money pit," Ben scoffed.

The house was entered by a single staircase, unlike most Barbadian plantation houses which had a double staircase. It had a ground floor with an arcade of flattened arches, and an upper floor surrounded by an open verandah. The house had a single hipped roof with two gable dormer windows, unusual in Barbados, but common in South Carolina.

Around the mansion, the tropical vegetation was taking back the land.

They went up to the door and knocked; it was dark and locked up tight.

"But it's for sale!" Alison complained.

"I don't imagine they'd mind us looking around the grounds," Ben said. "It being for sale and all."

Dan nodded. "Good thinking." He looked at the grandeur of the house and the surrounding area. "I can't believe the Graham family once owned this."

"The house would have overlooked rich fields of sugarcane," Alison said. She put her face up to the soft breeze. "We're nearly a thousand feet above sea level. Do you feel that breeze?"

"It's the trade winds," Ben said. "They constantly sweep across the island from the east."

"You can see the bright blue Caribbean sea in the distance," Dan said. He took a deep breath. He could smell the aroma of thick tropical vegetation, crumbling masonry, and the moss that grew everywhere.

They began strolling around the side of the house as monkeys chattered and jumped in the trees overhead.

"Barbados is probably one of the best and most moderate climates in the Caribbean," Ben said. "You know, its constant breezes cooling the air is the reason it has one of the largest White European populations in the Caribbean." He leaned over to peer into one of the windows.

"At these high altitudes," he said as they started walking again, "some of the sugar planters even had stone fireplaces in their homes to keep them warm in the winter. St. Nicholas Abbey, Bloomsbury, maybe even Drax Hall. They had them made from bricks that came over as ballast in the sailing ships. Although Barbados is tropical, up here, it can get quite chilly at night."

"You seem to know a lot about Barbados," Dan commented.

"We once thought of living here permanently. Maybe running a bed and breakfast."

Alison linked her arm through Ben's. "If we had enough money, we could buy this old plantation. Wouldn't that be marvellous?"

Coral Castle looked out to the blue and emerald-green tropical sea on its western side, and the lush green valleys and hills on its eastern side.

"What do you think of the view from up there?" Dan pointed to the gable dormer window high up.

"It would be magnificent, I think," Ben said. "But I fear if I lived here I would never get any work done."

"You could keep an eye on all that's going on below," Alison said. "That would have been handy during the cane-cutting season. But you'd be very exposed to the elements, I think, especially hurricanes." She shivered involuntarily.

"The sugar planter would have lived up here," Ben said. "There should be a windmill nearby. There would have also been the other plantation buildings and the huts for the slaves, indentured servants, and other workers. And also stables and other animal pens, for cows and oxen. They would have provided their own milk and meat."

"And manure for the fields," Alison added.

"Yes, they didn't just have sugarcane fields. They would have grown other vegetables and food stuffs." They looked over the fields.

Before they went past the house to explore the grounds, Dan looked over towards where the windmill site should have been and jumped. He thought that he saw a small pale face peeping at him from the foliage; the little face was looking right at him with haunting eyes. Dan felt an icy chill wash up his spine and his ears seemed suddenly muted.

"Are you coming, Dan?" Alison's voice broke the spell and the child disappeared. The window was dark and lifeless again. Dan turned away to follow Alison and Ben into the overgrown vegetation.

"It would have had its own watermill to pump up water from the coral stone caverns below," Ben was saying.

A keen environmentalist, Dan jumped into the conversation. "The sugar culture was a good example of a sustainable, environmentally pure industry. The windmill provided clean energy from wind power. The residue from the sugarcane stalk provided food for cattle and fuel to boil and produce the sugar. The cattle dung fertilized the fields. A perfect circle of rotation. Of course," he noted, "they also used Black slaves and White servants for free labour."

"Yes, Newcastle plantation used a lot of White servants to cut sugarcane," Ben observed. "That was because it was close to the poor White village of Martin's Bay. Even today they live predominantly on fishing and a bit of farming there."

"Some of them came up 'over the hill' over the years," Alison said. "Some successful White business owners today came from there."

Recently, a descendant of Oliver Cromwell and some Irish Catholic priests had come over to meet these people, as Cromwell had been largely responsible for transporting their ancestors as prisoners or political rebels from Scotland, Ireland, and England. After Cromwell had defeated the Irish men, he shipped their wives and daughters over to Barbados, where they were sold as White slaves to English sugar planters as wives and concubines; an Irishman or woman could be sold for seven pounds in Ireland and bought for ten to twenty pounds in Barbados.

They were about to turn around when Alison, who had ventured a bit ahead, called out, "I found it!"

Dan's heart went up into his throat. *The treasure?*

"The windmill!" she cried. The men strode quickly through the vegetation to join her. It was missing its blades but stood proudly, a tall, crumbling cylinder covered in vines and foliage. The door was missing and the dark archway beckoned them. Dan carefully pulled aside the leaves and stuck his head inside. The dim light filtering through the corroded stone showed only the shell remained. He heard a fluttering and a small squeaky sound above and quickly pulled his head out.

"Bats," he said.

Alison grimaced and stepped back. "Well, that's enough for me. We can probably start going back, I think."

"That's the boiling house," Ben said. They took a quick look. It was a huge rectangular building with a peaked roof. It had clearly seen better days.

"Makes me a bit sad," Alison said.

"Coral Castle would have many stories to tell of life in the Golden Age of King Sugar," Ben pronounced as they made their way back to the car. "Dances in the ballroom, dinner for many at the large mahogany table seating thirty people or more. I can only imagine what a great house this would have been in its heyday. But those days are long gone." They all looked solemnly at the crumbling mansion as they moved past it. "I imagine recent generations of owners, without their numerous slaves and servants, couldn't possibly cope with its decay and need for constant maintenance."

"So what do you think?" Dan asked Ben and Alison as they reached the car and got back in for the trip home. "Would you want to have lived in Coral Castle and enjoy the good life?"

Alison tilted her head, considering a moment. "Not really, I think." She turned in her seat to talk more directly to Dan. "Life in those days must have been very high society, with all that wealth. But I can't imagine the sugar planters going to the beach to have a swim or going off boating or suchlike. I think they just hung around the house, drinking rum nonstop, being nagged by their spouses, and constantly in fear that the slaves would revolt and kill them. The nearest neighbour was miles away. The sons were sent to school back in England. They might not see them for years, and by then, they'd be strangers. And what about the clothes? Ben," she said turning back to him, "you would hate to wear a three-piece all the time. They must have roasted in the hot weather. And you'd have to send your girls off to England to meet some rich Englishman."

"Or he might come over here," Dan said, "like Antoinette and her Englishman in *Wide Sargasso Sea*."

"Yes!" Alison said cheerily. "These West Indian-born women seemed to be sexier than their English counterparts, like Antoinette. Maybe that's why my English husband married me. Am I correct Ben?"

"Of course, my dear."

"Does it work in reverse too? Do West Indian-born men seem to be sexier than their English counterparts?" Dan asked.

Alison broke in. "Well Dan, it seemed to work in your case, as I remember when you were a teenager you had that English girlfriend from a very rich English family holidaying in Barbados—Denise."

"It did, pity she was only here for a short time, I was just getting to know her, I could have been a rich man today."

The rest of the ride passed amicably and soon Dan was climbing out of the car and wishing the couple a happy vacation.

"Let's not be strangers," Alison cried as they drove away. She stuck her head out the window to add, "Let's buy Coral Castle!"

Laughing, Dan headed into the building. When he got into his apartment, he pulled a cool drink out of the fridge and sat down on the balcony and called Aunt Mary. He updated her on meeting Angus and his Treasures. He was enjoying the cool breezes when his phone rang. Dan didn't recognize the number.

"Hello?" he asked in a friendly tone. "Who's this?"

"Why, laddie," said a Scottish voice loudly into the phone, "it's Angus!"

Dan frowned but kept his voice light. "Hey, Angus. How did you know my number?"

"Well, you told me you were staying in Rockley, didn't you?" Before Dan could point out that hardly made it easy to find him, Angus went on. "Just wanted to let you know I've had to cut my plans short. Family emergency. You know how that goes."

"But what about finding the treasure and rewarding the descendants and all that?"

"Oh, don't put too much stock in a drunk man's ramblings. There's probably no real treasure to find. Just some fantasy in the mind of an old history buff. Anyway, thought I'd let you know I'll be going back home tomorrow so you won't see me on the island. Have a great holiday."

"Sure, Angus. You have a safe trip."

Dan sat on the balcony a long time, until the sunset turned to moonlight as his mind turned over the events of the day.

CHAPTER FOUR
Unsealing the Past

The boy sat in his long white nightshirt on his little bed in the room under the eaves. He was small and pale for his ten years. In his hand he turned over the two prayer-bead bracelets again and again. They had once belonged to his mother and to his father. And when he touched the beads, he felt their presence.

He tensed suddenly and cocked his head to listen. He could hear heavy footsteps going up the stairs. The feet paused after hitting the sixth squeaky step. The little boy carefully blew out his candle, wrapped the prayer beads around his wrist, and crawled under his bed.

The little lipstick-red car stopped with a squeal of tires in front of Dan's apartment the next morning. His sister Jessica got out; she was the living image of their dad, with her brown hair and blue eyes.. She was very vivacious and happy and five years older than Dan.

"So you survived chatty Alison and dour Ben, did you?" Jessica asked by way of greeting. "Aunt Mary updated me on everything about the Cuthbert Treasures, so I am good to go on this exciting family mystery and treasure hunt."

They had a full day planned. They were off to the Archives to research Dan's family and the family of the missing boy, and family of the Scots prisoner. Then a jaunt to the famous west coast of Barbados to visit the ancient Church of St. James, which had some family tombs and other ancient artifacts. The west coast was also where the rich English entertainers and aristocrats had their winter homes. Then the siblings would visit Dan's favourite beaches from childhood.

The car sped down the Errol Barrow Highway to Warrens, winding past the D'Arcy Scott Roundabout, zooming down the Gordon Cummings Highway, past the University of the West Indies Cave Hill Campus, and then veering onto the road to the old Lazaretto building, where Jessica parked the car so quickly she made Dan lurch in his seat. He bit his tongue so as not to say anything. He still needed her to take him places.

The Archives were housed in old buildings of the British military establishment, which were once, in colonial days, used as a sanatorium for inmates who caught leprosy, hence the building's name, Lazaretto, after Lazarus, the biblical leper.

They entered through a gate that led to the old military buildings, with their wide verandahs running around the perimeter. The buildings had wide windows and doors to let in the tropical breezes, which cooled things off nicely for the people poring over the wills of great-great grandfathers and other assorted relatives.

The Barbados Archives facility was where all genealogical and other records were kept. Many of the records originated in the 1640s and were found in magnificent, leather-bound books, written in ancient copperplate script that recorded details of the births, deaths, marriages, and wills of ancient ancestors. The old books, recopied several times over the centuries, along with the accompanying mistakes in spelling and other inaccuracies intact, were kept on shelves open to the breezes. It wasn't a simple matter to track down families, as spelling of names could change over the generations. However, they provided a fascinating record of life in one of England's oldest colonies.

Jessica and Dan greeted the custodian of the old registers, who was sitting behind a little desk at the door.

"Hi," Jessica said confidently. "We're tracking down some family information and would like to look in the archives."

He was an ancient Barbadian, who obviously took great pride in his domain. He looked at them with an assessing eye as if they'd come in to

Unsealing the Past

damage his precious charges. After getting more information from them about what they were looking for, the old man handed them a piece of paper and gestured them towards another desk where another Barbadian, the librarian, sat. The other man, who was also old—*Perhaps it's a prerequisite of the job*, Dan thought—walked down to the stacks and returned, gleaming with satisfaction and enthusiasm, an old register in his hands.

The register was quite heavy and about two feet by two feet, and three inches thick. It was blue and tied up with string. The cover showed copperplate writing. There were several of these books, the Parochial Register Index, the Deeds Register, the Wills Register, the Marriages Register, and the Baptisms Register, all dating before 1800.

Dan and Jessica were directed towards eight wooden tables where a mix of people were seated as they conducted research. The ceiling in the research room was very high and, at the two ends of the room, at the very top, two little round windows that could be opened by a rope at ground level were open to let in cross breezes. The pages of the old registers occasionally turned, as the breezes made their way across the room. It was either that, or ghosts.

As they found a table and sat down, they heard a cooing from above, and a pigeon flew in through one of the open round windows. It flapped its wings and then settled on a high perch near the ceiling. They would be looking for the record of Dan's earliest ancestor in Barbados.

In the records, Dan flipped through the pages until he found the name of an ancestor in Barbados.

"Jessica," he said. "Look here. Robert Graham. His son shows up in the census of 1679. But here's his father's will the year he was buried in 1677 in Christ Church parish church on 2nd July 1677"so this was the information that he needed to take to Christ Church, to try to find the grave.

"I've got some paper ready," Jessica said. "Let me get down that date. We'll need it when we go look for his grave."

He couldn't find the original deed for Devon Farm, but instead he saw an early deed dated 18 July 1674 where he read, "'Robert and Joane Graham of Christ Church sold Henry Welch, 5 acres of his plantation in Christ Church, bound north by George Reid, Harold Lane, east, David

Bourne, south, and Paul Taylor, west." This would have been Devon Farm before it got its name.

The pigeon cooed and then swept low across the heads of the people at the tables. One or two screamed. Then it settled itself on top of a stack.

This would have been the first deed that Dan could find on his direct ancestor.

"It would seem like deeds before 1640 are not in the book," Jessica said. "So we can't see the original land purchase."

Another pigeon flew in through the open window.

"I'm going to get another register," Jessica said. "See what else we can find." As she stood, however, the second pigeon flew towards her. She shrieked and ducked.

"I'm going to take some notes over there," Dan said, pointing towards the side of the room. However, before he could take any notes, the custodian was in the room, issuing an order to close the books. They had to remove the birds before they hurt anything. The birds were Ramier pigeons, with slate-grey bodies and purplish-red heads and breasts, foreigners to Barbados and native to Dominica.

Jessica and Dan moved under the archway, hoping it would be over soon so they could continue their research.

The pigeons had now flown up to the top of the room and perched on the two little windows, one at each end. A handyman came in with a twenty-foot stepladder, which he placed against the wall. When he started to climb up to the pigeons, one pigeon promptly dive bombed him, splattering poop as it flew away to the other side. The handyman swore and ducked, and then climbed back down the ladder. He moved the ladder to the other side, and tried again. But as he climbed to the top again both pigeons flew across the room, dive bombing him and letting off another white stream of poop.

The custodian of the books cried out in shock to see his old books now vulnerable to assault from the air and urged the handyman, "Man, hurry up, and lick dem blasted pigeons down."

The handyman pulled on the ropes to get the little round windows open at the top and said, "Dere, you can fly back to Dominica for all I care." But the pigeons just settled down on their perches.

He went and got an old empty cardboard box and with great stealth crept back up the ladder. Then with a lunge forward, he tried to trap the pigeons in the box.

There was a great noise and a loosening of feathers, which floated down through the air, and swearing from the handyman, but somehow the pigeons escaped and flew back across the room.

"Medford, what de hell yuh think yuh doing, man? You can't treat birds like dat. Dem is pigeons."

Everyone turned to look at the speaker. It was the big boss from the Ministry of Public Works.

"Shall we go?" Jessica whispered to Dan. "This looks like it could take a while. And I don't think I want to watch poor Medford get in more trouble."

Before they left the Archives, they turned back to see the Ministry boss creeping up the ladder with the box while the custodian, librarian, and handyman urged him on from below.

"In Barbados, you can always count on the unexpected," Jessica said. "Maybe we can come back tomorrow."

They drove along the coast towards St. James Parish Church. Being on the leeward side of the island, the sea was much calmer on the west coast of Barbados. It was now home to many very wealthy people, such as famous English entertainers. There were expensive hotels and the famous, world-class Sandy Lane Resort.

"That's where Tiger Woods had his wedding reception," Jessica pointed out.

"Not on the golf course, I hope," Dan joked.

Along this coast, they passed the village of Paynes Bay and Holders Hill, the home of the Barbados Polo Club. The first horse polo match in Barbados had taken place in 1884 and was a very popular sport among the sugar planters and rich merchants.

They sped into Holetown and passed the obelisk monument that commemorated the landing of the first English settlers, incorrectly stating 1605—Captain John Powell claimed the island for the king in 1625 and the English settlers didn't arrive until 1627.

They arrived at St. James Parish Church, where Dan had gone to church in his youth while staying with a cousin who lived on a plantation nearby. It was the oldest church on the island, built near the site of the first English settlement in 1627. The original church and a subsequent church had been destroyed by a hurricane.

The current church was built in 1874. It had natural coral stone walls, circular columns, a circular bell tower, carved spiral wooden staircase, and stained-glass windows. In the southern porch of the church, on a pedestal, sat an ancient black bell inscribed with "God Bless King William–1696." It had been erected fifty-four years before the famous Liberty Bell of America. There was also a baptismal font erected in 1684.

In the churchyard, Jessica and Dan found a number of big stone vaults of Grahams, the Bristol branch of the family. They were the big plantocrats who had taken their emancipation monies and gone to the new colonies of Australia and New Zealand, where they were able to buy ten times the acreage they had in Barbados. The vaults were all in a state of decay and covered in wild tropical vines. Despite searching throughout the site, they found no graves that were early enough for the Coral Castle Grahams. But it was lovely walking through the grounds nonetheless. A famous Barbadian, who had met with Benjamin Franklin twice in Paris to deal with the effects of the American Revolution on Barbados, was buried in this graveyard. This Barbadian was also a friend of Olaudah Equiano, the Black Abolitionist, and was mentioned in Equiano's autobiography.

They spent a few hours relaxing at the Folkestone Marine Park, a lovely little cove for easy swimming, snorkelling, kayaking, and paddleboarding. It had an artificial reef nearby created by the sinking of the SS *Stavronikita*, an already-damaged Greek freighter, in 1978. This little cove with its calm and gentle waters was a popular destination for local Barbadians. Dan had spent a lot of time there in his youth.

On the way back he watched the scenery, but his mind was puzzling over the mysteries.

The first mystery was the death of the little boy and what had happened to his parents, the boy himself, and his cousin. The cousin was Dan's ancestor and they had all died under mysterious circumstances. He wanted to see the documents transferring Coral Castle to the lawyer.

The second mystery was what had happened to the lawyer who took over Coral Castle.

The third mystery was whether Coral Castle and Angus's Coral Gables were, in fact, the same place.

And if so, that brought him to the fourth mystery: did the deaths of his ancestors have anything to do with the St. Cuthbert Treasures, stolen by the Scot prisoner Montagu, was the lawyer involved, and where was the treasure now? Despite Angus's phone call, he was beginning to believe firmly in the Treasures.

As they passed the Archives, Dan suddenly said, "Turn around, Jessica! Let's do another search."

"I'm not sure how long they'll still be open," she said, looking at the sky. But she made a sharp U-turn and pulled into the Lazaretto.

On entering, they saw the custodian and waved. He smiled slightly this time and looked harassed. "You have two hours," he said.

They were moved into a different area than before.

"Still having bird problems?" Dan asked.

"We are looking for a more permanent solution," the custodian said in a clipped manner.

Jessica raised her eyebrows at Dan so he kept any follow-up to himself. But he couldn't help murmuring, "Glad I'm not a bird."

The custodian ushered them into the microfiche room. It was air conditioned to the point of iciness.

"Man, it feels like the North Pole," Dan said.

"Yes, sir, everybody ask that question," the custodian said impatiently. "You en de first, but we have to keep it that way to preserve the records."

"Ok, but maybe you should tell people that they need a sweater."

The man looked at him evenly. "Usually researchers come here from cold countries, searching their Barbadian ancestors. They is accustomed to the cold already. Where you all come from?"

"I come from Canada, but not the cold part, but I'm Bajan born. When someone comes down here they're looking for hot, not cold."

"I am sure you won't be in here long," the custodian said, lifting his chin slightly. "Outside is very warm."

With that he closed the door and left. Jessica audibly let out her breath. "I see you're still bringing your charm to everyone here in Barbados."

"Let's just start searching. You look for the letters of administration that passed Coral Castle to the lawyer Mulroney. I'm going to look up Montagu."

They scanned as quickly as they could, checking their watches periodically and calling out time.

"Dan! Over here!" Dan went running over. "I found a document referring to a Sean Mulroney," Jessica said. "In 1736 he sells a plantation called Coral Castle to a Rupert Allen for 33,000 British pounds. That must be the lawyer! His name is Sean Mulroney."

"Great stuff, sis. Here, I'll write that down."

"And it shows William Graham died on September 3, 1706, leaving the plantation to Joseph Graham. That must be the little boy." *Was that the child I saw in the foliage?* "I'll see if I can find anything else about Sean Mulroney."

Dan shifted his search to St. John Parish records and found a reference to Hugh. "Jessica," he called out, "I found a burial record for the indentured servant Hugh Montagu. He died in December 1680." He frowned. "But that can't be. He has to fight the Frenchies at St. Kitts in 1689."

The custodian walked by and coughed. It was very close to closing. Dan and Jessica tried to work faster.

"Dan," Jessica gasped. "Look at this."

He took it and read out, "'Hugh ye son of Hugh Montagu, and Maureen Yates a pore white woman 5th October 1671.'" He looked up. "He had a son. A son named Hugh. I was looking for a burial, not a baptism."

"So based on this," Jessica said, "the original Hugh Montagu could not have gone to St. Kitts. Hugh Junior was nine years old when his father died. He could have gone to St. Kitts in 1691; he would have been twenty years old."

"Hugh Montagu and Maureen Yates. Sounds like they weren't married. Did you look for a marriage records?"

"Doesn't seem to be here. What if…"—Dan frowned as his mind tried to make connections—"the Grahams at Coral Castle became the guardian of Hugh's nine-year-old son? Could William Graham of Coral Castle

Unsealing the Past

also have been the guardian of the stolen St. Cuthbert Treasures? Would Hugh, the father, have entrusted his employer to keep the treasures safe for his son?"

"Could that explain all the mysterious deaths?" Jessica asked. "Could it all be because of the St. Cuthbert Treasures?"

"This is big."

Jessica nodded.

The custodian came into the room and announced it was time to close.

"We had a productive day," Dan told him happily. "We'll uncover the mystery of Coral Castle yet if I have anything to do with it."

The custodian lifted his eyebrows in surprise.

"What?" Dan asked suspiciously.

"Nothing," he replied, firmly keeping his lips tight.

"Was someone else asking about Coral Castle?" Jessica asked.

The custodian shifted away his eyes and announced once again it was time to close. Dan wanted to argue, but it looked like the man had had a very trying day.

"Birds still there?" Dan asked.

The custodian simply pursed his lips. Realizing they'd get nothing more out of him, Dan and Jessica thanked him and soon the door was shutting firmly behind them.

As they sped back down the highway in the little red car, Dan felt more optimistic than ever. "We found some good stuff," he said to Jessica. "But who else is researching the Coral Castle plantation?"

"Do you think your Angus is still here?"

"Maybe. But then why would he bother calling me and say he was leaving?"

"I think we need to search faster."

As Jessica was dropping him off at his apartment, Dan had an idea. "Do you want to see if John would like to help us tomorrow at the Barbados Museum and Historical Society Library?" Dan had told John about the St. Cuthbert Treasures.

"Sure, I'll call him tonight," she said. "Three eyes are better than two. But, I'm just warning you," she added. "We'll have to feed him"

53

***

The next day brought rain as a tropical depression passed through. Rain pounded the little red car as it sped along.

"It'll be a good day to be indoors," John said as he listened to the rhythmic sounds of the window wipers. Then he shook his head. "This climate change thing is really screwing up the weather." He was sitting in the back seat of the car, fastidiously removing his rain hat and brushing the rain off his coat. He took off his glasses and wiped them with a cloth.

"Tell me about it," Dan said. "The sea has come all the way up in Worthing. It now touches the walls of my grandfather's old house. We've got to stop it before it does more damage."

"So the itinerary today," Jessica said loudly over the drumming of the rain, "is the Barbados Museum and Historical Society. We should look in newspapers, censuses, ship manifests, militia rolls, anything that will shed light on Hugh Montagu. We'll look at the Shilstone Library."

The Shilstone Library was housed in a building of the old military prison, part of the Garrison, a complex of old military buildings situated around a big, circular open grass field, where horse racing regularly took place around a circular track.

At the south end was the old military fort of St. Anne's. It was built in the early eighteenth century and had a fortress-like wall with old cannon emplacements. On the west end was the Savannah Club, which had an ancient clock tower with a clock like Big Ben in England. In front of the Savannah sat a collection of seventeenth-century cannons, one of the oldest and rarest collections of seventeenth-century English iron cannons in the world.

The entrance to the museum library was on the right of the main museum, guarded by two old seventeenth-century cannons stuck in concrete.

The group made their way to the library, passing through security and facing a narrow flight of stairs. On either side were stained-glass window portraits of hallowed English kings, and the coats of arms of old members of the Barbados parliament.

Unsealing the Past

At the top of the flight of narrow stairs was the Shilstone Library, named after Eustace Maxwell Shilstone, a Barbadian historical researcher. They entered into a small narrow room. Around the edges of the room were bookcases full of books, filing cabinets, and other materials, containing historical records and other documents available for research. Ladders hung on the walls to access the books and documents at the highest levels of the book cases.

They greeted the custodian/research helper sitting behind a desk.

"Good morning," the librarian said, "and welcome to our library. It's a good day for research."

Like all things in Barbados, it was very official, with lots of forms for them to complete to get any of the documents they wanted. But everyone was very polite.

"Let's break up the research," Jessica said.

"I'll be looking for the boy and his father, and Cousin Robert," Dan said. He found himself starting to think obsessively of the little boy who had died.

"Jessica and I can look for anything on the lawyer Mulroney and Hugh Montagu," John said.

"Sure thing," she replied a little tentatively.

Dan found a synopsis of Barbados history that had been written by a family member a long time ago and given to the library. He had always been proud of the history of Barbados, as he felt his ancestors who settled there in 1628 had not conquered anyone or stolen the land from anyone, unlike in North America. He was sitting at his own table, his resources spread out in front of him. Jessica and John had their own table with most of the books stacked in front of John. Dan looked over at Jessica. She rolled her eyes a little.

Chuckling, he started reading Barbados history and was just getting into the flow of the old fashioned wording, when he heard a voice call out too loudly for a library.

"What's a pirate doing in a library!"

"Pirate?" Dan asked.

"Don't tell me you forget you stole my girlfriend!"

"Stephen?" Now he could see another Worthing boy he'd got in trouble with in his teens. Stephen was a tall, wiry Barbadian, with green eyes and hair receding and lots of sun freckles from the hot Bajan sun.

"In the flesh."

"How are you, my man?"

"Still pining for my girlfriend." Then he squinted his eyes and pursed his lips. "What was her name?"

He said, "Andrea" just as Dan said, "Adelaide," and then they both laughed and said, "Doreen!" together.

"So, are you looking for a pirate ancestor of yours or some criminal ancestor from England?"

Dan smiled. Stephen was an amateur genealogist and always did get right to the point.

"I'm looking for the guy who was rich as hell then lost it all before it could ever come to me."

"Sounds like a mystery."

"It sure is," Dan looked back to his papers and frowned.

"Well, make sure that you share some with me and don't forget all the things I did for you in Barbados growing up."

"I won't. You should make a list, what are you doing here?" Dan asked him.

"Just passing through," Stephen said enigmatically. He waved to Jessica, who waved back with a wide smile, then he gave Dan a wink and was off back down the stairs.

Dan leaned forward to continue reading.

"The island was empty when the first English settlers landed," his ancestor had written, "and the only life on the island were some pigs that the Portuguese had left to provide food for any shipwrecked sailors."

While the Arawak Indigenous people had lived there once, it was empty of people when the English arrived. The Arawaks were peace-loving people compared to the warlike Carib Indians.

In the seventeenth and early eighteenth century, Barbados was the richest and most developed British colony, whose wealth and influence had at one point exceeded the thirteen British colonies on the American mainland. This was because of sugar.

Unsealing the Past

Even in religion Barbados was ahead of the America
addition to its Anglican churches it had the first Jewish
Western Hemisphere, the Nidhe Israel synagogue in Br
lished in 1654, while the first American synagogue was lai

"Guess what I discovered," John continued, tilting his ͟͞au, "that one Sean Mulroney was listed in the census of 1715 of all White persons in Barbados; however—"

"—there were *no* Mulroneys on the list of slave compensation payments in 1838," Jessica finished. "So the Sean Mulroney family must have left the island for good."

Dan learned that Barbadians had settled South Carolina after 1670, particularly in Goose Creek. There slavery was also encouraged; prospective settlers were given free land if they owned slaves, and in this way they could become prominent planters. This seemed to coincide with Mulroney's disappearance from the Barbados records. South Carolina and Goose Creek looked like a good place to start looking for Mulroney.

Dan looked over to where John was talking with Jessica, though it looked like John was doing most of the talking. With a little snicker, Dan decided to go give her some air.

"So, John, Jessica," he said as he approached their table, "let's compare notes. What have you found out? Anything juicy?"

"Of course," John said, "I found quite a lot."

Jessica leaned forward in her seat. "*We've* found quite a lot."

"Yes, my dear," John answered dismissively while Jessica sighed. "Firstly, I found that the owner of Coral Castle had five White indentured servants; however—"

Jessica cut in, "—Hugh Montagu does *not* appear in the 1715 census; that means no Hugh Montagu, father or son, was on the island then. We know the dad was already dead. John figures Hugh Junior must either have died, left Barbados, or never came back from St. Kitts." She patted John's arm.

Dan tried to hide his smile. John seemed torn between being mollified by Jessica's attention and miffed at her usurping of his story.

"Shall we work together on the militia lists?" Dan asked. "See if we can find Montagu junior there?"

57

As they worked, Dan was amazed that John could carry on a conversation about one thing while researching another. As they searched, he lectured them on the history of Barbados. It didn't matter that Dan kept reminding him he was from Barbados.

"And so William Pitt the Younger," John was saying, "stated in 1798 that the annual income from the West Indian colonies, which included Barbados, was four million British pounds as compared to one million British pounds from all the other colonies. We were very well off." He paused to make a note about what he was reading on a pad of paper.

"Pitt argued that little Barbados, a mere 166 square miles, was more valuable to British capitalism than the vastly larger colonies of New England, New York, and Pennsylvania combined. In fact, the Barbados census of 1679 is said to be the only complete census of any British colony at that time, and it reflects a very rich colony. Barbados had its first university, Codrington College started construction in 1714 and opened in 1745."

"Even as late as 1752," John said, continuing with a raised voice, already going on to the next subject, "George Washington, the first American president, went to Barbados, to 'see the bright lights of a city,' and to learn the intensive planting methods being used in Barbados to bring back to Virginia to improve his plantations. "Barbados is the only country that Washington ever visited outside of the United States, the house where he stayed in Barbados is now a museum."

"That Americans owe us everything," Dan responded as Jessica snorted with laughter. "Prince Hall was a Black Barbadian who set up the oldest African-American freemasons lodge in the USA in 1784."

"In fact," Jessica said, "a few Americans of Barbadian descent signed the Declaration of Independence." She leaned towards her brother and said in a loud whisper, "I paid attention in history class."

Records indicate that up to 30,000 Barbadians of all colours emigrated to the American colonies prior to 1700, so many early Americans have Barbadian roots—"

"Which brings us round to Mulroney again," Dan finished.

Jessica clapped her hands in appreciation. "You did that neatly."

"Aha!" John said. His finger was pointing to the page of the militia lists. Dan and Jessica leaned over in excitement. "The Regiment of Foot from St. John's Parish. One Hugh Montagu. That would be Hugh the junior. And here, the list shows a William Graham of Coral Castle supplying five men to the regiment."

"Oh, John, you did it!" Jessica cried, squeezing him in a one-armed hug.

"This confirms," Dan said, "that Hugh Montagu the senior was an indentured servant at Coral Castle plantation and—"

"—*not* Coral Gables," they all said together.

John continued scanning the pages. "This is interesting." Once again Jessica and Dan leaned in, but John waved them back a bit. "There was another Regiment of Foot commanded by a Colonel Timothy Thornhill—"

"That's the name Angus mentioned," Dan exclaimed, "Sir Timothy Thorn-something!"

"Yes, he was the commander of the Barbadian forces that later conquered St. Kitts. Let's see, in the 1679/80 list, the regiment was composed of 655 men. Hugh Montagu was a pikeman."

"Hugh Montagu was conscripted into it for the St. Kitts expedition. That's what Angus said."

"So the expedition to St. Kitts must have also included men from other regiments besides Sir Timothy's," John said, stroking his chin in thought. "Where does Sean Mulroney fit into all of this?"

He pulled over the stack of newspaper records. "We need to look through these. Look for anything after 1715 that mentions Mulroney." His stomach interrupted with a loud rumbling. "Then I am afraid we will have exhausted my stomach's patience."

Dan's stomach rumbled in response, and Jessica laughed. "The male stomach," she said. "We'll make sure to get them fed."

After furiously scanning the papers to the ever-increasing sound of John's stomach, they hit pay dirt. The *Barbados Gazette*, the first newspaper of Barbados, had a story about an atrocious murder in Bridgetown in 1732 by a lawyer called Mulroney. He was indicted but pardoned because of friends in high places. This led the three researchers back to the ship lists where, with a cry of discovery, they found a list of ships and settlers to early South Carolina with a Sean Mulroney, barrister, on the barquentine *Endeavour* journeying to Carolina on October 9, 1736.

Dan sat back in his seat. "So Mulroney was a bad man."

"And the Montagu mystery is connected to Coral Castle," John added.

"He stole the plantation," Jessica said. "Do you think he took the St. Cuthbert Treasures too?"

"Treasure." Dan nodded. Then he laughed and hugged Jessica. "There's treasure!"

"I told you we had a mystery on our hands," she replied.

"We're on a treasure hunt now." He clapped his hands. Then he turned to John. "But first, let's get your stomach some food."

When he got back to his apartment for the evening, Dan fired up his computer to research Angus's story: the Battle of Dunbar, Durham Cathedral, the Cromwellian era, and especially the St. Cuthbert Treasures.

Before he dropped off, he thought of the little ghostly boy in the foliage. "Good night, Joseph," he mumbled. "Stay safe."

CHAPTER FIVE
Ghosts and Churchyards

The door flung open and slammed into the wall. The man was holding a candle in his hand. It was shaking slightly and he smelled of rum. Sweat glistened on his forehead and his hair was plastered on his head.

"Where are you, little boy?" he asked in a sing-song voice.

The boy pushed himself farther under the bed and made no sound.

"I've had enough of you," the man slurred. "I'm a real daddy now." He gestured wildly with his candle. "I don't need you anymore." He turned to look at the open doorway. "Shh," he whispered with a slight giggle and quietly shut the door.

Armed with the information he'd collected from the Archives and his research, Dan waited outside for his ride. A dusty blue car came zooming up and stopped with a lurch.

"No Jessica today?" Dan asked, leaning down towards the open driver's window.

"She sends her regrets," his niece Silvia said with a cheeky smile. "Something about swimming and piano, but I think it's a cover for a date."

Dan climbed into the car. "A date? Who with?"

"I'm not sure. I think there's someone new, but she won't tell me about it."

Dan looked concerned. "Should I be worried? Why aren't you asking her about it? Is this being responsible?"

Silvia laughed, put the car in drive and sped off with another lurch.

"Did your mother teach you to drive?" he asked.

"Yes," she said. "You should be happy that it's not Jack driving you." Dan's shoulder hit the passenger door as she took a fast turn. "She taught us both."

Today they were going to explore the old churchyard of Christ Church, where the earliest gravesites of his family should be found. It was by Dover Beach, a wide beach with strong sea currents. It was a now popular spot for water sports like windsurfing and jet skiing.

This was the first Christ Church parish church; it was then rebuilt four times over the years. The first church was built in 1629, about two years after the first English settlement was established in Barbados. In 1669 a storm of heavy rains and floods destroyed the church and washed most of the wooden coffins out to sea; only the stone vaults remained. According to an eyewitness at the time, "It was a dismal spectacle to see with the coffins standing up on each side of the banks of the beach, and enough to make one think of the Resurrection."

The second church was built later, this time high on a hill at least a mile from the sea; that too was destroyed by the great hurricane of 1780. Rebuilt in 1786 on the same hilly location, it was destroyed again by the great hurricane of 1831. It was rebuilt again in 1835, but then destroyed by fire in 1935; then it was rebuilt for a fourth and final time.

Dan and Silvia got out of the car and moved towards the site of the first graveyard, which held the oldest gravestones. There were only four vaults left for the four oldest families. The oldest one was a husband and wife named Adams. No Grahams.

"Our first family members must have been buried in a wooden coffins," Dan said, "and been washed out to sea in the 1669 storm."

Dan looked around the space. Besides the four vaults, the graveyard was empty. There was the avenue of Pride of India trees, with their pink blossoms, the new Sandals Resort for tourists on one side, and the Hotel Bougainvillea on the other—both on one of the most beautiful south coast beaches of Barbados, Dover Beach. But despite this beauty, the graveyard looked a little lonely. His thoughts strayed to a little boy, many years ago.

He shook himself out of his reverie and said to Silvia, "Let's try the more recent graveyard up the hill. Maybe we'll find a family member there."

They piled back into the car and zoomed to higher ground, along the ABC Highway, past the Foundation school, where another of his great-great-grandfathers had been school headmaster in 1890, past suburbs, situated on the first of a series of ridges that made up Barbados, rising up from ground level at the coast to a thousand foot peak mid-island.

The second Christ Church parish church had been built on the first ridge. The view was magnificent. Silvia stopped the dusty blue car for a moment at the top so they could appreciate the green fields and villages in the distance and, further on, the light green and darker blue of the sea.

The ridge also overlooked the seaside village of Oistins, a name that evolved out of the corruption of Austin's, an early landowner. Some of his descendants also gave their name to Austin, Texas, when they settled there by way of South Carolina. It was a popular name. Oistins was also the home of the famous fish festival.

"I wouldn't mind getting some flying fish," Dan said, his mouth watering at the thought.

Silvia laughed, "Some things never change, Uncle Dan."

She turned the car into the entrance of the church and swung around the circular driveway. They pulled into a parking spot and climbed out of the car. The breeze up on the ridge was fresh and strong.

The church looked like a castle, with an imposing tower and crenellations turned black with age. Three of the walls and the west tower had survived from the 1800s. On the one side was a graveyard of old stones dating before the nineteenth century. The modern graveyard, from the 1900s onward, was on the other side of the church. They went in through the front door and were met with the cool inside air. They stopped for a moment while their eyes acclimatized to the dark.

"Can I help you?" a woman asked. She was standing by the church office and offering a welcoming smile.

"We're looking for some ancestors," Silvia said. "My Uncle Dan is visiting from Canada."

"Canada, *eh*?" the woman asked, pleased with herself. As she prattled on about her ties to Canada through a cousin of some neighbour, she walked them out to the graveyard on the right side of the church.

"This is where the oldest graves are," she said; by now they knew her name was Irene. She looked around at the stones and vaults. Vegetation was growing all over them; some were crumbling. "It's unfortunate that so many of these family vaults are in very poor condition." Yet the graveyard had an air of serenity. "Good luck," Irene said and left them to their search.

Most of the inscriptions were no longer legible. When the slaves were emancipated in 1838, about eighty percent of the sugar planters took their emancipation money and left Barbados. With no family remaining in Barbados, the old vaults and tombs had fallen into decay.

They searched everywhere. They tried Dan's random I've-got-a-feeling-it's-here-approach and then Silvia's systematic accountant-like grid search, but they finally had to admit, "There are no Grahams here."

"Why aren't they here?" Dan asked. "We found Robert's will; they were God-fearing, staunch Church of England people. Well, Silvia, do you think it's time to call it quits?"

"Looks that way," she said scanning the graveyard, squinting her eyes as if a gravestone would pop out of hiding. "We've searched everywhere, and given it our best shot, so we shouldn't feel bad about quitting."

"Wanna look for the Chase vault?" Dan asked. "Get spooky?"

"Sure," Silvia said, "I'm up for a little ghost walk. At least we can say that we saw that this trip."

The Chase vault was the most famous coffin mystery of Barbados. It was in the oldest section of the churchyard and was now blackened with age. The vault was wide and squat and built out of coral stone with concrete walls. A small staircase led to a yawning doorway with two small blank windows on either side of the doorway. It looked like a face. An illegible coat of arms of the Chase family was carved on the outside above the doorway. The doorway had once been closed with a ponderous slab of Devonshire marble.

The vault dated back to the 1700s when James Elliot built it for his wife. Then it changed hands to another family and, in 1807, Mrs. Thomasina Goddard was first entombed there. They discovered at the time that the

Elliot coffin was no longer there. The vault changed hands again to the Chase family. Little two-year-old Ann Maria Chase was entombed there in 1808 and then her older sister, Dorcas, in 1812. Only a month after Dorcas, Thomas Chase himself died and the tomb was unsealed. They found the coffins tossed about the vault like a child's playthings—this, though some of the coffins were made of lead and took six people to lift them. The infant's coffin was upside down across the little room. They righted the coffins, entombed Thomas, and sealed the vault back up. Four years later, another infant was buried. When they moved the marble slab from the doorway, they found the same thing had happened again. There was no evidence that the entrance had been forced.

Silvia and Dan moved down the steps to peer into the dark gloom of the vault.

"I still find this scary though there's no coffins left inside," Silvia whispered, her voice echoing into the empty room. In 1820, after the governor opened the vault and the coffins were again in disarray, the family requested that the coffins be removed and buried in different graves in the churchyard.

"There has never been a plausible explanation," Dan said in a low voice. "The lead coffins were too heavy to have floated in water, though there was no sign of flood. There had been no earthquake activity in the area. The slaves said it was a supernatural agency at work."

Silvia shivered. "I can believe it." Dan gave her a one-armed hug.

"It even smells funny," Dan said. He made a big shiver and sniffed the air. "Could it be rotting flesh?"

"Uncle Dan!" she admonished. "You're just trying to scare me." But his attention was caught by something in the dark-shadowed corners of the vault. Was something moving? This time he really did shiver and goose bumps raised up and down his arms.

"Who's that man?" Silvia said sharply. Dan jumped.

"In the back corner?" he whispered, his voice unnaturally high.

"No," she said with a frown. "Him." She was pointing to someone across the graveyard. "He seems to be watching us."

As Dan turned around to look across the graveyard, he saw a man duck behind a gravestone.

"That's not natural," he said. "He's definitely watching us." He put an arm around his niece as if to protect her, though the man was nowhere near them. He tried to think of how they would get to their car safely.

"It's okay, Uncle Dan," Silvia said. "I took a women's self-defence course." She pulled out her keys and bundled them into a tight fist with the key facing outward, then she whispered "Hammer strike!" and swung the key downward followed by a "groin kick" with her knee.

"Jeez, Silvi," Dan said, moving carefully away from her, "you're scaring me. Let's just run to the car, okay?" He took a couple tentative steps up the vault stairs, keeping his eye trained on the gravestone across the yard, when the man ran out from behind the stone, moving quickly away from them. Dan widened his eyes in surprise. "Angus?" He started up the steps. "Hey, Angus!" and started running. But the Scotsman was running as fast as he could around the corner of the church.

"Uncle Dan?" Silvia called. She started running after him.

"Angus!" Dan yelled. "What the hell are you doing?"

"Uncle Dan! Do you know that man!"

"Yes, he's a sneaky Scot."

"I'll get him!" and she took off like a shot, moving towards the church and disappearing around the corner.

Suddenly there was scream.

"Silvi!" Horrified that he hadn't stopped her, his heart pounding, Dan put on a burst of speed and rounded the corner. He slammed into a big, solid body and fell to the ground. He looked up to see—

"Tarzan?"

"Who is that?" The man was standing like a six-foot rock, his arms folded, glowering down at Dan. Silvia was standing next to him talking animatedly with—

"Siggy?"

"Dan!" She reached a hand down and pulled him to his feet.

"What are you doing here?" Dan demanded. "Where's Angus? What do you have to do with Angus?"

"Uncle Dan," Silvia said coming forward. "I'm sorry to scare you. It was so stupid, I rounded the corner and ran right into these people. They said the man ran past them and has gone off in his car. They're here sightseeing

Ghosts and Churchyards

and I'm so embarrassed for running into them. You know these people?" she finished on one breath.

"Did you know that man?" Siggy asked.

Dan rubbed his head. "Uh, yeah, we've met. Just some drunk I met at the Crane Hotel." He thought it best not to talk about treasure. "We're both looking for long-lost relatives and it looks like our paths just crossed. He's actually supposed to be out of town." He added with a mutter, "Playing games, I think."

Then he turned to Tarzan and stuck out his hand. "Sorry, pal, I mean, Al, hope I didn't hurt you."

Tarzan just smirked in reply and kept his arms folded.

"What family are you looking for?" Siggy asked, her face bright with interest. She smiled reassuringly and Dan felt his ears go a little pink.

"Well," he said, "the Grahams were once wealthy planters. The plantation that's for sale, Coral Castle?" He leaned in. "It has its own mystery attached." Then he lowered his voice, "But that's just between you and me."

"Uh, Uncle Dan?" Silvia said. Dan looked up. She rolled her eyes towards Tarzan, who looked like he might just throw a punch any second.

"But," Dan said, taking a large step back and putting on a jaunty air, "it's time for me and Silvi here to get back on the road. Lots of touring to do before sundown."

Silvia slipped her arm through his and steered him away from Siggy. "Nice to meet you!" she said with a big smile and a wave. When they were far enough away, she scolded her uncle. "You were drooling all over her in front of her boyfriend. Her very large, built-like-a-rock boyfriend."

"I think he has slow-firing synapses," Dan said with a frown, turning with a big smile to wave at Siggy.

"My mom's told me stories about you, Uncle Dan." She shook her head. "I guess they're all true."

On the way back along the ridge, they passed the location where Devon Farm, Dan's ancestor's place used to be located in the 1850s. It was now a cricket sports field.

It had been another frustrating day and a bit sad. Dan thought of all those people buried in the old part of the churchyard whose descendants now lived in other countries. They probably never even knew that these ancestors and vaults existed. He could see why the ghosts got a little fed up sometimes; if he were a ghost, he'd throw his coffin around.

But, he wondered, *what was Angus playing at? Why was he still on the island? Why had he bothered calling at all? And where was the treasure?*

They were rather quiet as they drove back along the ABC Highway, passing by the little villages of St. Lawrence, Graham Hall Terrace, Worthing, and finally Rockley. The little dusty blue car stopped with a lurch in front of his apartment.

"Well, Uncle Dan," Silvia said, "life is never dull around you."

"That is true," he said with a tired smile.

"Tomorrow Jack's taking a turn at driving you around." She winked. "Don't eat too much for breakfast."

CHAPTER SIX
Pirates and Thieves

"So how are you enjoying yourself so far?" Jack yelled above the roar of the car's engine. Jack was Dan's nephew, a very fit-looking, handsome, tall lad with brown hair and blue eyes.

They were driving in Jack's slick new bright blue sports car with the top down. Dan was holding on to the door handle, his hair blowing into his eyes, lurching this way and that from the speed, cursing the fact he'd pooh-poohed Silvia's advice and eaten a full breakfast of eggs, bacon, and toast.

"Quite," he said, closing his eyes for a moment as a fresh wave of nausea set in. "I've never focused so much on the history of Barbados and our family."

Their tour that day would cover many of his old favourite spots: Bathsheba on the east coast, where they'd check out his old bay house in Hillview; lunch at the nearby Atlantis Hotel; and a visit to Codrington College, to see if there was any trace of their scholarly ancestor. Codrington College was located in the island's interior in St. John Parish near Coral Castle.

They were speeding down the Errol Barrow Highway, named after the first premier of Barbados at Independence in 1966. They would then go northeast at the Bussa roundabout.

The roundabout was named after a slave who led the slave insurrection in 1816. Though the rebellion had failed—many Blacks lost their lives and others were hanged or transported to Africa—the rebellion shook the Barbados slave-based society to its core. While slavery had been abolished by the British in 1807, the institution itself had remained and the Barbados Slave Code of 1661, a series of laws for governing Black slaves, stayed in effect. It was recently noted on CNN TV that the Barbados Slave Code, brought by the Barbados settlers to South Carolina, became the basis of slavery in the Southern USA.

Bussa and the others thought that the Barbadian sugar planters were rejecting abolition and if they wanted freedom, they had to take it by force. The roundabout commemorated this event with a statue of Bussa breaking the chains of slavery that bound him.

Heading northeast past Bussa, they passed through the beautiful St. George Valley, a wide expanse of open country, with green sugarcane fields, small forests, the occasional plantation house, and a sprinkling of churches. They passed villages filled with colourful chattel houses—small wooden houses that weren't anchored to the ground and could be moved as, historically, their owners didn't own the land the houses sat on.

They zoomed past rum shops and other small businesses, and small gardens of vibrant orangey-red flamboyant trees, with their tangle of trunks and limbs, and bougainvillea vines of white, pink, orange, purple, and red.

Their first stop would be Codrington College, which was built in 1745 to rival Yale and Harvard. It was the oldest Anglican theological college in the Western Hemisphere. When early Barbadian Christopher Codrington died in 1710, he left portions of his sugar estates and land in Barbados and Barbuda to the Society for the Propagation of the Gospel in Foreign Parts, a Church of England missionary organization, to establish a religious college in Barbados. He also left 4,500 British pounds and about 12,000 books to his alma mater, All Souls College, in Oxford, England, where the Codrington Library still exists to this day.

Jack turned the car into the long avenue of majestic royal palm trees. On the grounds off to either side were species of giant silk cotton trees with their buttress roots twisting above ground; white cedars and mahogany; fan-shaped traveller's palms, so named as the sheath of the stems would collect water for parched travellers; and festively red flamboyants.

They murmured their appreciation of the large pond filled with lilies and ducks. The college overlooked the parish of St. John and, beyond, the blue Caribbean Sea.

Dan shook his head. "With that view, I'd never be able to concentrate on studying."

"It sure is beautiful," Jack agreed. "I can smell the ocean." The royal palms fluttered in the breeze above them as they drew up to the college and parked the car.

"Looking for anything particular, Uncle Dan?" Jack asked as he got out of his car, wiping a smudge off the car's hood.

"I don't know," Dan said pursing his lips. He looked at the imposing school; it had been designed after Oxford University. Three tall arches of coral limestone covered an open space with a checkboard stone floor. The arches sat below three tall windows, which in turn sat below a massive cross. It was originally built as a grammar school to prepare young Barbadians for universities in England.

"I never knew we had a connection to the college," Dan said to Jack. "Maybe it's important." He looked up at the massive cross of Jesus. "Let's go in and just look around."

As they entered the chapel, Dan felt a cold shiver run up his spine. "In here," he whispered. The room was intimate, not a large size, and overwhelmingly covered in rich red cordia wood. The ceilings were vaulted, and all eyes were brought to the cross of Jesus hanging above the altar. Dan sat for a moment on one of the pews that lined the centre aisle as Jack wandered around the room. He closed his eyes and absorbed the peace of the room for a moment, putting aside the pressing questions about the past. He started to feel … transcendent … and that's when he felt the brush of a sleeve and a soft voice whisper in his ear, *"He lies without and looks up to God."*

"Uncle Dan?"

Dan opened his eyes with a start.

"I think this was a little too peaceful for you," Jack said, smiling. "You fell asleep."

"Yeah," Dan mumbled. "Maybe … " He looked around the chapel but it now felt merely serene and beautiful. "Let's go," he said.

They climbed into the car and drove down the driveway, the royal palms waving them through. They got back on the highway. It was a quick, eight-mile trip to St. John's Church, which sat high on a hill with an incredible view of the little bays along the coastline, like Consett Bay, Martins Bay, and Congor Bay.

As they turned a corner on the winding road, Jack yelled, "Ahh!" and swerved onto the shoulder as a black car came right at them on the wrong side of the road. The black car passed in a blur without stopping.

Jack pulled the car back onto the road and slowed down considerably. Both their hearts were pumping furiously. "Damn American," Jack snarled, "or Canadian drivers. Don't understand that we drive on the left side of the road. In Barbados you drive on the left." He looking accusingly at Dan, who lifted his hands in surrender.

"Don't get mad at me. I'm Barbadian too."

There were no further mishaps and they were soon approaching the church, which sat among plantations on the rugged east coast. The original church was a wooden structure that burned down. And like St. James Church, successive churches did not survive the series of hurricanes. The current church was its fifth incarnation, built in 1836, with the chancel being added forty years later. Its gothic style was very imposing. The entrance was through a square tower four-storeys tall with arched portals on three sides. The top of the tower and the surrounding roofline were crenelated, like a castle.

Dan was on a mission. He led Jack around the side to the back of the church where the cemetery was. Here the vaults and gravestones were well preserved. There were famous denizens, like Ferdinando Paleologus, one of the last members of the Palaiologos Dynasty, which had ruled the Byzantine Empire—the Christian emperors of Greece. His father had fled to England in the late sixteenth century after the Turks conquered Constantinople; he married an English woman, Mary Balls. Ferdinando moved to Barbados and was an early settler of the parish of St. John, where the Balls owned property. His memorial in the graveyard was a popular feature. Looks like he angliscized his surname.

"Just imagine a Greek nobleman in Barbados; apparently when the Greeks wanted to restore the Greek monarchy they came to find any descendants of Ferdinando, but could find none," said Dan.

Behind Ferdinando's memorial was another popular grave: the grave of Thomas Hughes, who was buried standing up, at his request.

Dan and Jack began looking through the old tombstones.

"Here they are, Uncle Dan!" Jack said, gesturing to an area of old tombstones. The extended Graham family was buried there; there were a lot of them, going all the way back to the 1600s and 1700s, but no William Graham or Joseph Graham. "He lies without and looks up to God," Dan said. "Does that mean anything to you?"

"No," Jack answered. "Is it a quote?"

"You could say that." Dan crouched to look at an old gravestone. It was a Graham child who died young, both the name and date had been erased by age.It must be very, very old," he sighed. "So many died so young, didn't they?" He stood up again and said abruptly. "Go to the Atlantis? I could do with some sea air, the beautiful view, and more importantly, fish cakes."

The road passed through Newcastle plantation, one of the few places in Barbados where poor White workers were active cutting sugarcane, as Newcastle was near the redleg village of Martins Bay. These people were sometimes called Backra, because they sat in the back row of churches, as Whites were seated in the church according to their status.

They passed the little Anglican church of St. Margaret's. It was built in 1862 by the Haynes family, the owner of Newcastle plantation; its congregation was predominantly poor Whites. The road took them past Foster Hall's Andromeda Botanic Gardens. It was designed by botanist Iris Bannochie in 1954 as a family retreat with over 600 plant specimens, and gifted to the Barbados National trust on her death in 1988.

Before they stopped at the Atlantis Restaurant, Dan wanted to check out his old family bayhouse, the summer house by the sea. Their bayhouse was named Hillview. It sat on a high plain overlooking the east coast of Barbados in the seaside village of Bathsheba.

"Jack, keep your eyes peeled. I remember this area. We're getting close." He sat forward in his seat, nostalgia fuelling his excitement.

Hillview was built by Dan's father on the site of an old hotel called Beachmount. The driveway was an avenue of casuarina trees. In front of the house were five acres of open land running down to the cliff overlooking the railway tracks.

The bayhouse had a wonderful view from a wide verandah. Cool on a hot day, the verandah looked over, on one side, the whole village of

Bathsheba and the wild Atlantic surf, and on the other side, Tent Bay with its colourful fishing boats. Back in the day, they had been sailboats instead of power boats. At sunset, the colourful sailboats of the fishing fleet would wind their way through a narrow gap in the reef to return to their safe haven in the village of Tent Bay. There was also a stream near the house that brought fresh water down from the mountainous cliff; Dan used to fish for crayfish there as a boy.

In the late 1980s to early '90s, a group of archeologists financed by Cambridge University did a survey of the area of the stream and surrounding land in front of the house and discovered Indigenous pottery from the Saladoid period dating to about 300 AD. Thousands of pottery sherds were found, as well as marine shells (which turned out to be early tools) and fish bones. The pottery was quite beautiful.

The house was no longer in their family.

"Jack, stop!" Dan shouted as the house came into view. It still had the casuarina trees lining the drive. The house was now a tropical blue with white trim and red roof. The little lawn was smooth and green. He knew that beyond the house, below the cliff face, past the long curving beach, very similar to the California or Oregon coast beaches, the wild Atlantic surf pounded several rock formations that had been eroded over the years by the waves, very much like Cannon Beach, on the Oregon coast, now one of Dan's favourite places.

"That's a beautiful house, Uncle Dan."

"I remember long walks on the beach, and swimming in the wild surf and sea pools. We'd hike up the surrounding hills and along the old railway tracks. Our family would pile into the car and go visit little picturesque coves. That was, of course, way before computers. I remember playing all sorts of family games, indoors and outdoors." His voice dropped to a wistful tone. "Those were fun days." He smiled at the memory of it.

"You know," he added, "all those cottages and vacation homes along the long strip of beach have names."

"That's cool."

Dan nodded. "Enough reminiscing," he said abruptly. "Let's go to the Atlantis."

The Atlantis was a small, intimate hotel sitting at the bottom of the cove. It was built in the 1800s along the railroad tracks that would bring Barbadian holiday makers from Bridgetown. It only had eight bedrooms with large windows opening up to the sea breezes. Constant landslides ended the old railway's lifespan in the 1940s.

They parked and got out of the car.

"We can sit on the upper storey verandah," Jack said. "That's pretty nice."

"I'm definitely ordering a rum punch," Dan said.

Both their heads turned as a yellow mini Moke went speeding by. Dan only had eyes for the beautiful woman behind the wheel. A black car was following close behind.

"Antoinette!" Dan shouted.

"The black car!" Jack said.

"What black car?" Dan asked.

"The one that nearly killed us. Who's Antoinette?"

Dan shrugged in an embarrassed way. "Just someone I met at the beach who I'd like to get to know better."

"Hope you're successful, Uncle Dan. Her car looks pretty cool."

Dan laughed and slapped his nephew on the back. They made their way into the restaurant.

"Welcome to the Atlantis Restaurant," the hostess said cheerfully. "We're open daily for breakfast, lunch, and dinner, with our famous West Indian buffet every Wednesday and Sunday." She took a breath and smiled, showing a dimple. "It's very popular with both locals and visitors. Our menu is authentic Barbadian and Caribbean cuisine, and we only use the freshest local ingredients. If you'd like to book the restaurant for a special occasion, we can seat more than 200 people on the inside and outside decks. Usually we strongly recommend reservations, but you're in luck today. Follow me," she added perkily. She gestured towards the buffet. "Enjoy."

The men followed her to their seats on the upper verandah. It was a beautiful spot, with a constant, refreshing sea breeze; a hush of swaying coconut palms; and the crashing of the waves. They enjoyed a rum punch as they looked at the Atlantis sea pool opposite, across the tracks.

"I used to stand on the big rock in the centre of that pool," Dan said gesturing, "and wait for an incoming wave to force its way in between the rocks. Then I'd dive into the white foam as the wave passed by." He took a swallow of rum. "Great fun. I never had any problem sleeping then."

"When I was younger," Jack said, "I'd surf here." He nodded towards the few surfers that were out in the water. "Tent Bay's now the surfing capital of Barbados. Bathsheba has a whole new group of residents from the international surfing community."

"I heard that a local surfer was killed."

"Yeah, he was surfing the big waves," Jack said. "Just before a hurricane warning." He shook his head. "He was only seventeen. Broke his neck after he was thrown onto the reef, I knew the guy, it was quite sad."

Dan sighed, and became aware of the aroma of the buffet, the smell of the ocean, the noise of the waves, and the chattering of the people. With the magnificent view of the ocean, it was almost too much to take in. "Okay, let's feast."

Dan walked past the serving tables and helped himself to the soup of the day to start; it was Bajan fish soup. When that was done, he went back for more—the famous spicy Bajan fish cakes in the zesty pepper sauce; the famous Bajan flying fish trio of blackened, grilled, and fried flying fish; garlic and herb potato wedges; and coleslaw. He followed that with coconut cream pie with Malibu rum sauce for dessert.

"Heavenly," he said on a sigh. "The whole buffet was one helluva spread."

"Have you seen Coral Castle lately?" Jack asked. Dan looked up from his pie and coffee. "Alison was talking to Mom about it."

"It's a real pity it's been left to fall apart. Must have been magnificent in its day."

" Alison wants to restore it."

"It would cost a lot of money."

"Yeah, but she can't seem to get it out of her mind, she told Mom."

Dan took a thoughtful sip of coffee. "Seems to be going around."

"Well, maybe one of these days someone will restore it," Jack said.

"Can I ask you something?" Dan said.

"Sure." Jack pushed his plate aside and leaned forward. "Shoot."

"Do you believe in ghosts?"

Jack raised his eyebrows. "Not what I was expecting. Usually the family hassles me about getting married." He lowered his voice. "Where did you see the ghost? At the Castle? Did you see the little boy?"

"You know about him?"

Jack took another sip of coffee. "I've heard the legend. Never saw him myself, mind you." He frowned a bit. "But I think people see things when they're meant to."

Dan leaned forward and whispered, "I saw him."

Jack tilted his head. "Then maybe he wants something from you."

Dan nodded his head. "Well, that gives me a lot to think about."

The journey back home took them up steep, twisting hills with forests full of banana trees. When Dan was a teenager, he'd had a small, convertible Morris Minor English car, which had manual gearshift. He'd have to change gears three times, ending up in the lowest gear, to make it up the big hill, Horse Hill, to get back home. Jack's convertible zoomed up it effortlessly.

The passed the old Round House. Sporting round walls in part of the house, hence its name, Round House was built in the 1850s as a private residence along the railroad. In more recent years it had been converted to a restaurant with some guest rooms.

Soon they were back in the parish of St. George, driving past the Gun Hill Signal station, one of four points where guns were placed to signal enemy ships or the like; it had a large white English lion carved out of solid coral rock by an English officer.

They drove past the old St. George's parish church, built in 1640, which featured a large painting about Jesus's resurrection called "Rise to Power," painted by American artist Benjamin West about 1776.

The painting was commissioned by sugar planter Henry Frere and exhibited at the Royal Academy in London. When it landed in Barbados, Frere had an argument with the rector, and as a result the painting wasn't hung. It was stored in an outbuilding on the sugar estate where a thief, during a robbery, saw the Roman Centurion in the painting staring at him and stuck his finger in the eye. The damaged painting was sent back to England for repair but, as no artist would repair it, a black patch was painted over the eye. It was sent back to Barbados and eventually hung in the church, black patch and all.

"One of our ancestors was the headmaster of St. George's parish school next to the church," Dan said, "just after slavery ended, another one was headmaster of Foundation school close to Devon Farm, that's why we Grahams are so smart, only joking."

"I wonder what they thought about the pirate patch in the painting," Jack replied.

Dan shook his head in wonder. "Pirates and thieves."

CHAPTER SEVEN
White Knight

The man dug the hole well into the night, the moonlight the only illumination he dared to have. Someone was always watching. When it was deep enough, he threw the lifeless body into the small hole with barely a glance. Shovel by shovel the dirt covered the little white sleeping shirt. As the dirt hit a small hand something flashed by the moonlight. The boy was wearing the prayer bead bracelets.

The man almost took the prayer beads off the wrist, but feared the sacred relics. The dirt shifted of its own accord and he quickly looked to make sure the child was dead, but the sightless eyes seemed to be gazing upward. In spite of himself, the man looked up as well.

He shivered. For a moment he thought he saw the cross of Jesus.

One of the loveliest Barbadian beaches on the south coast was where Dan's grandfather had lived in a house on Worthing Beach. Since his grandfather was blind in his later years, Dan would bring him to the water's edge, sit him down, and let the little waves come in and surround him for a sea bath. Dan's grandfather was a pillar of one of the Barbados churches.

He looked up along the beach. The beach was about a mile long, anchored on the west end by a local hotel, Cacrabank, sitting atop a rocky promontory. On the east end was another promontory on which sat the ancient St. Lawrence Anglican Church.

The Cacrabank promontory separated two beautiful beaches: on this side, Worthing Beach; on the other side, Accra Beach or Rockley. One beach was only accessible to the other by walking around the big promontory at low tide or by a little road. They were both beautiful white sandy beaches, with bright emerald-green water and white puffy waves breaking on the coral reef far out.

The promontory was a haven for fishermen catching tarpon, bonito, red snapper, and even barracuda from a perch on the rock.

In between Cacrabank and St. Lawrence Church was a lovely, undulating, pinkish-white sandy beach, with the emerald-green Caribbean sea lapping at its edges. It was where Dan was giving his feet a sea bath. He started walking eastward.

At low tide on the sheltered east end, you could walk onto the reef and turn the rocks over to see all the little denizens of the sea, including small octopus—"sea cats," as locals called them—sea spiders; sea eggs (or sea urchins); cobblers, which were black sea urchins with long spikes; and other weird and wonderful creatures of the deep. There were also conger eels, with their electrical shock.

He was going to meet Tommy today at the Carib Beach Bar, down towards the eastern end of the beach. It was good to reconnect with his past. The bar was at the end of a gap among houses where a lot of his beach bum friends were born, including Tommy and Stephen. Stephen, of course, was now living in British Columbia but visited Barbados often in winter.

As Dan approached, Tommy stood up and waved. He'd grabbed a table on the beach. The Carib also had a circular outdoor bar under cover with more tables. The site was surrounded by coconut trees with a sprinkling of almond trees. At night this would be lit up with strings of white lights.

"Remember when there was a house here?" Tommy asked by way of greeting. "Before the bar was built. Remember how we'd sit on the beach under the stars and watch outdoor movies?" Clearly he was feeling nostalgic too.

"Yeah, they were projected on a screen on the beach. They put the projector on the balcony." Dan smiled. "We spent a lot of Friday nights doing that."

"Didn't have to pay a dime either." Tommy shook his head. "What nice people. A Black family and one of the first Black millionaires in Barbados."

In later years Black Barbadians had become the major political force in Barbados in the House of Assembly and a growing force in the economy of the island.

"We watched some epic movies, for sure. Hey, remember," Dan said, pointing to Tommy. "*Island in the Sun*? It was filmed here in Barbados."

"Yeah, in the film a brown man, Belafonte fell in love with a white woman and they had a fit in the United States. Wasn't it banned in the US Deep South?"

They went to the bar, got a couple of beers, and settled back down.

"I feel like my whole childhood growing up on Worthing Beach was one big epic adventure. Didn't realize it at the time," Dan said.

"Time," Tommy said thoughtfully. "Makes you see what you lost."

"We had year-round summer weather, warm water, and sunshine. We fished for sprats, and swam and dived and surfed, dug for shells."

"How about beach cricket?"

"Yeah, beach cricket!"

"And what about those beach girls, wuhloss, those beach girls?"

Both men took a drink of beer and smiled.

"Remember the day that new one arrived?" Dan asked. "The one that came from somewhere else? Boy did she take the beach by storm."

"She looked like that babe in *Baywatch*. The blonde with the … " They both nodded.

"There were also those foreign girls," Dan said, "the tourists. Nothing like a little bit of foreign beauty to make life more interesting."

"So true," Tommy agreed. "A touch of foreign beauty passing through. Maybe your mystery beach girl Antionette is looking to enjoy herself to the fullest while she's here in Barbados." He leaned in. "And do things that she wouldn't do at home."

Dan shrugged non-committedly. "It was all good clean fun under the sun, no funny stuff, no tiptoeing through the two lips, if you know what I mean."

"Those were the good ole days, my friend," Tommy said mournfully. "And remember America had California and the Beach Boys, and we had Barbados and the Merrymen, with the leader from Worthing Beach?" He grabbed his beer like a mike and started singing, *Well I asked my lady, What must I do to make her honest and keep love true—*"

"*—She said, The only thing that I want from you is a little, little piece of the big bamboo*," Dan sang in answer. They both broke out laughing and high fived.

"Remember me playing the harmonica?" Dan said, tearing up a bit. "And, you, as I recall—"

"On the banjo or guitar." Tommy demonstrated with a little air guitar.

"Remember making those little wooden body boards to catch the big waves?"

"That was April Easter vacation, in the big spring tides—"

"And at Accra—"

"That was before the big fibreglass surfboards were invented."

"We were bad ass."

"Those were the good old days, my friend," Tommy said. "I continued to enjoy them, you know, while you went to cold Canada."

Dan sighed. "Growing up in Barbados we sure got to see a lot more skin year-round than in Canada. While my body was in Canada, I think my mind and soul were still here."

Tommy's cell phone beeped. He checked his text.

"Damn. Sorry, gotta split. I've got a tour client." He smiled apologetically. "I need the money." He got up and reached out to shake Dan's hand. "This was a lot of fun. Let's do this again soon." He walked down the beach and then turned and shouted, "You should watch *Baywatch*! I downloaded the whole series!"

"Stephen is here too, I saw him at the museum library," Dan shouted.

Dan laughed and waved. He shifted his chair to get a better view of the water and began "cooling out," taking it easy, listening to Caribbean calypso music being played on the radio. Sitting there, drinking his beer, sitting in front of the breakwater at a nearby resort, he felt happy, whole.

As an announcer broke in with a weather report, warning of a tropical depression, he watched two girls out on the exposed coral reef. They both had long dark hair and well-tanned, olive skins. One of the girls was very slim and tall and extremely well proportioned. The other girl was a bit on the heavy side and much shorter. They seemed to be arguing and the tall one pointed down to the ground and then at the other girl.

He laughed and took another sip of beer. *Why argue on such a beautiful day?* It was one of those perfect Caribbean days of brilliant sunshine and bright-blue sky with a few puffy white clouds, the smell of suntan oil and cream and seaweed permeating the air, and the sound of the waves lapping the shore and crashing on the coral reef. It was as about perfect as you could make it.

The girls, still talking animatedly, continued their walk down the reef when suddenly the shorter girl cried out and fell down to the rocks of the reef, clearly holding her right foot. The other girl looked towards the beach, right at Dan, and started screaming, "Help! Help us!"

Dan dropped his beer, kicked off his shoes, threw his watch and cell phone onto the table, calling to the bar staff, "Watch my stuff!" and, without another thought, ran across the beach and into the sea. He plunged in and swam as fast as he could, with sure steady strokes honed in his youth, towards the reef. He quickly pulled himself up onto the reef and carefully walked his way over the sharp rocks, making sure not to step on any cobblers, the local black sea urchins that inhabited the reef. These little crustaceans had hundreds of sharp spines that would enter the bottom of your foot. When he was a kid it would take them weeks to extract the spines with hot candle wax.

Dan heard the girls speaking in Spanish and crying, both looking down at the girl's foot, their hair covering their faces.

"*Buenas dias,*" Dan said, approaching them. "Can I help you?"

The girls looked up.

"Antoinette!" Dan said in surprise. His *Wide Sargasso Sea* beauty was standing over her injured friend.

"Dan!" Antoinette cried. Dan couldn't help but puff out his chest. *She remembered my name!* "Mercedes has been bitten by a most horrible sea creature," she said in her lovely accented English.

"Let me see," he said walking over carefully so as not to scare the women. The woman on the ground was crying, but she also looked a little angry. He reached down and carefully examined her foot. "Looks like the sting from a lionfish. See, there's a small hole." It was bleeding profusely. "This should have immediate medical attention," he said. "Are you allergic to lionfish venom?"

"She might be," Antoinette said quickly.

"I might be," the other woman said, angrily.

"She needs medical attention," Antoinette cut in, "or she could be paralysed or worse."

"We gotta go immediately," he said. He scooped the injured woman into his arms. She was unfortunately heavier than she looked. "Antoinette, help me lift her over the reef. I'm going to swim you back to the beach fast," he said looking down into her wet eyes.

"I am going to swim ahead," Antoinette said, "and call an ambulance."

With Antoinette helping to cradle the woman and lift her weight, they carefully walked to the edge of reef. He couldn't see where he was putting his feet, as he navigated over the sharp coral rocks, slippery sea moss, black cobblers, and other spiny creatures.

But Antoinette gave him such a welcoming look that it fired up his adrenaline and he made swift progress over the reef, finally lowering their weight into the water.

His feet were sore and bruised, and his back ached by the time he reached the shallow water. But the tide helped him to float her ashore. Antoinette had run ahead and an ambulance was called. He placed the woman in his arms gently on the beach.

"They'll be here in a minute," a voice said above him.

He looked up and for a moment was lost in appreciation of Antoinette's statuesque beauty: those eyes, that hair, and those curves. He momentarily forgot his sore feet and tired limbs.

"I am Maria," she said, finally introducing herself, "and this is my friend Mercedes from Caracas," pointing to the injured girl, lying on the beach. Mercedes looked at him with more of a pout than a smile.

Maria, on the other hand, knelt down and took Dan's hand. "Thank you so much, Dan. You are so kind. What can I do to repay you?"

Dan looked into her eyes and knew that his dream had come true. He thought of many ways in which he could be repaid.

"Is this the patient?" called out a strong male voice. The cavalry had arrived. One man was bald; the other seemed to have a lot of hair tucked under a misshapen hat.

They loaded Mercedes into the ambulance, and as Maria was about to leave with them, Dan called out, "We should get together!" Maria turned back to look at him. "You know, to update me on Mercedes's health," he added, "because I'm so concerned about her."

Maria smiled. "Just call the Sandy Lane Resort and ask for Maria."

As the ambulance pulled away, Dan rolled her name on his tongue as he went back to the Carib to retrieve his stuff. "Maria. Marrrria." But in his mind, she remained his Antoinette.

***

He waited three hours before giving in and calling the Sandy Lane Resort.

"How is Mercedes?" he asked once he was patched through to Maria.

"She's doing fine, thanks to you," her voice purred.

"Would you like to have dinner with me tonight? I thought we could go to Champers."

"Yes I'd like to, thank you again. Your quick action might well have saved her life," she said earnestly.

"No big deal, Maria." He stood up a little taller as he spoke. "Anyone would have done the same thing."

"But no one did," she pointed out. "I will see you there at six."

"Uh, sure!" He nearly dropped his phone.

"Till then," she purred and hung up.

Dan ran into the bathroom to get ready for his date.

Champers, which used to be called Torrington, was one of Dan's favourite restaurants. It sat high on the promontory in a little curved gap between Worthing and Accra Beaches.

How lucky can a guy get? he thought as he scrubbed his hair in the steaming shower. *A little vacation romance.*

Champers served local fare as well as international dishes. He thought Maria might be Venezuelan. *They're exotic beauties*, he thought. *She might like their exotic fare.* Dan thought about the menu and what Maria might like. The restaurant offered appetizers like hot soup, poached calamari salad, camembert, spring rolls, Caesar salad, shrimp and mango salad, crab crêpes, coconut shrimp and chili sauce, and duck breast and apple salad. For the main course, she could have Cajun blackened dolphin, the famous Bajan fried flying fish, or Scottish smoked salmon. *I haven't come all this way to have Scottish smoked* salmon, he thought as he started shaving. Just thinking about it, his stomach rumbled, and he suddenly realized how hungry he was.

At six sharp, he was waiting outside the restaurant. He could smell the aroma of the food and hear the sound of the waves below him crashing on the rocks below him. The sun was glinting on the water and on the waves in front of him. There were a few surfers out on this wonderful day.

The little yellow Mini Moke pulled into the parking lot and Maria stepped out. She was wearing a loose-fitting sun dress with a plunging neckline, a pearl necklace, and on her feet, little strappy high-heeled sandals.

"Hi Maria," he said, enjoying how the name felt on his tongue. "Great to see you again. How's Mercedes?"

"Doing great."

They went inside and the hostess led them to a table with a magnificent view of the water.

"Is this table suitable?" he asked.

"Yes, it really has a wonderful view."

As they sat and looked at the menu, Dan suddenly felt a little awkward. Maybe it was Maria's beauty. He searched around for an opening line. "So Maria," he said, "tell me a little about yourself. Are you Venezuelan?"

"No." She smiled shyly. "I was born in Barbados and went to school at the Ursuline Convent, so many of my friends are Venezuelan. They were sent to the convent to learn English. I learned some Spanish from them."

"So you're Bajan born and bred?"

"Well born, yes, but I don't know about the bred part."

The server came to the table and Dan ordered a round of rum punches.

"I'm a very mixed-up girl," Maria said, continuing the conversation. "I have all kinds of different blood. My mother's family was from Trinidad and had Carib Indian, Black, Spanish, Jewish, and English, all mixed up in there, maybe even a little Chinese too. My mother is very protective of me," she added with a shy smile. "On my dad's side there's White … and some Black."

"Well," Dan said, smiling, "I was sure you were Spanish. It's great that you learned a second language, especially in a tourist area like Barbados."

When the server came back with the drinks, Dan ordered the Bajan flying fish and a mango and shrimp salad, and Maria ordered the Cajun blackened dolphin and a Caesar salad.

"The dolphin, of course, is also known as mahi-mahi," Maria said after the server had gone. "It sometimes upsets the tourists," she said with a shrug.

The food was delicious, the view from their elevated table overlooking both beaches was fabulous, and the cane-backed chairs around each little table were very tropical looking. With the amazing circular view of the sea and the cool breezes coming in, this was destined to be a great date. Yet, something wasn't working. Dan tried to extract more information about Maria's family, to get to know her better, but after her first comments, she seemed to always turn the conversation back to Dan.

"Tell me a bit about yourself," she asked as their meals were served.

"I was also born in Barbados. I moved to Canada when was I was nineteen. I have two daughters, Sarah and Michelle, both grown up. I was married, now divorced, and now I live in West Vancouver on the west coast of Canada."

"I hear it's cold over there."

"Not as cold as the east coast."

"So what are you doing here," she asked, "besides saving young women from peril?"

He laughed. "Well, to be honest, I am trying to solve an old family mystery."

"Ooh," she said, her eyes sparkling, "that sounds exciting."

Then he talked about Coral Castle, the mystery of the little boy named Joseph. The evil Sean Mulroney.

"Did you know Coral Castle is up for sale?" At his surprised look, she added, "I work as a property manager and real estate agent for Sandy Lane."

"Ah, so did you know about the family legends?"

"About the mysterious deaths?"

"Yes."

"No. It sounds fascinating."

To pique her interest even more, he told her about meeting Angus Montagu and his tales of treasure.

"You mean to tell me that there may be hidden treasure somewhere on this island that belonged to some poor white redleg guy called Montagu? That's really something. And an evil Sean Mulroney." She squinted her eyes in thought. "I used to know a mixed race girl at school who was named Montagu. None of them were rich."

"I think I saw you zipping by the Atlantis the other day," Dan said. "Were you showing a house?"

Maria's cell phone beeped and she checked her text. "Oh, no," she said. "I'm so sorry. I have to go urgently to meet with a client on the west coast." She stood up and gave Dan a quick kiss on the cheek. "Thank you for dinner. Again, I'm sorry. I can't keep these rich clients waiting." She stood up and gathered her purse. "Call me soon and let's go for a swim."

With that, and a lovely wink and smile, she made her way quickly to the little Mini Moke and was gone.

Dan sat back in his chair. "Darn it," he muttered and signalled the server for the bill.

CHAPTER EIGHT
Mad Dogs and Englishmen

The man walked a complete circle around the young girl; his eyes gleamed wickedly as he looked her up and down.

"She's very ... appealing," he finally said.

The other man stood frowning.

"Sean, you said you'd treat her well."

Sean gave the man a mocking look. "I said I'd pay you well. I always treat my slaves the same ... better than they deserve."

He lifted a lock of her hair and smelled it. She shivered and looked at her old master with frightened eyes.

"Maybe I should take her back home," the other man said.

"Robert, go home," Sean said. "The deal is done."

Once the man had left, Sean called to his man servant.

"I need your help getting rid of a problem. But first, I need you to get me a snake."

Dan woke up the next morning and found himself in the middle of a raging storm. The winds were blowing violently against the shuttered windows, and the rain crashed down on the metal galvanized roofs of nearby houses.

Brilliant flashes of lightning lit up the windows and the loud roll of thunder crashed around him. It had arrived in the still of the night.

Sunset the evening before had been quite beautiful; it was unusual in its fiery pink and orange colours, tinged with shades of grey. The clouds had been puffy and white, like marshmallows.

A tropical depression had been forecast. They were pretty common between the months of July and September, but they weren't in hurricane season yet, it was only June. The old doggerel of *June too soon, July stand by, August it must, September remember, October all over* was now totally wrong; climate change was screwing up everything.

"Soon we'll be having hurricanes in winter," Dan muttered.

He grabbed his camera and headed down to the beach to record the storm. The sea was wild, with big waves and boiling surf crashing right up against the walls of the beachside houses; the storm surge had obviously started. Soon the waves would be smashing into houses and kitchens and flooding right across the main road. He turned his video onto a coconut tree that the wind was trying to uproot; the sand around it was being swept away. The wind pushed against his back; it was a strange feeling, but somehow exciting and stimulating all the same, a bit like early winter storms in a northern climate, but without the cold.

A beach umbrella abandoned on the beach below him was suddenly ripped out of the ground and sailed through the air uncomfortably close. If he'd been two inches over, he might have been impaled.

There were two hearty souls trying to swim in the water. They must be tourists. They had trouble even getting into the water, with the constant pounding of the waves. It looked like no fun at all. One after another, the waves rose up. The people either had to swim fast towards the wave or swim fast in the opposite direction so the white-foamed wave wouldn't crash down on them with all its energy.

Dan switched his phone over to the weather station. The tropical depression had been upgraded to a hurricane. He watched as the swimmers grabbed hands and ran out of the water just before a big six-footer wave crashed down on them.

He heard a crash and the coconut tree finally fell over. He decided to get back to the apartment before he got himself killed.

In his boyhood days, Dan had always felt safe in their big house, called Erindale. It had eighteen-inch thick, coral stone walls that could withstand the greatest punishment. The old windows had inside and outside shutters to protect the glass panes; the roof had a parapet around it to prevent the wind from getting under the shingles and ripping them off.

Hurricanes had come frequently to Barbados in the past—1650, 1700, 1780, 1831, and 1898—and the people had learned by trial and error how to build houses that provided protection. In his youth, when a hurricane was all over, young Dan would sneak out the house, against the advice of his mother and sister, to look at the devastation, which was usually widespread, with felled trees and greenery everywhere.

Now as he was making his way back to the apartment he heard a loud barking behind him. He turned and saw a huge Great Dane jump over the fence of a house and charge towards him.

He looked up at the coconut trees, but since he hadn't climbed a coconut tree in years, he ran like hell. He remembered that his apartment had a pool and ran towards it. He scrambled over a small fence, threw his phone into the bushes, and jumped right into the big pool. Churned up by the strong winds, the water buffeted him around. The dog followed, clearing the fence in one swift jump, and landing at the side of the pool. It began a low, menacing growl.

"I guess you can't wait to take a piece of my ass," Dan said to the dog. "Sorry to disappoint you, but you're going to have to stick to dog chow tonight."

Meanwhile, the apartment building owner saw what was going on and came running out. He grabbed the hose and turned it on full blast on the dog. It snapped at the water a few times, turned tail, and with a running start, leapt back over the fence.

"Thank you, Keith. Man, you saved my life. Why would anyone own a mad dog like that?" Dan said.

"Well in Barbados, mad dogs are everywhere," Keith joked. "The Englishmen have left, but their mad dogs are still here, though it's not quite the midday sun."

"Cute," Dan said. He swam to the ladder through the whipped-up waves. The building owner helped pull him out and he went to the bushes to find his phone. As he headed back round to the front of his building, examining the bruises on his arms and legs from his mad scramble over the fence, he barely noticed that four frogs, which had been cavorting in a rain puddle in the road in front of his building, had been electrocuted by a fallen wire. The wind almost pulled him into the puddle, but he threw himself towards the door of his building and safely got inside.

"I would hate to go to the Pearly Gates earlier than planned," he said aloud.

Dan stayed hunkered down in his apartment throughout the day, eating bread and fruit and whatever didn't need heat as the power was out. The last weather report he'd heard said that the hurricane was changing direction again and the brunt of it was only hitting the eastern part of Barbados.

As he lay in bed, listening to the high winds, his last thoughts were about Coral Castle. He hoped it survived the storm.

Next morning, he woke up and went out onto the balcony. Everything was calm. There were a few downed trees and coconut palm fronds, branches, leaves, and flowers thrown all over the place, but the only physical damage that he could see was a loose piece of galvanized iron roofing that had blown off a neighbour's roof and a few uprooted trees. A crew was already fixing the downed powerline.

He turned on the news to hear there was some major damage on the east coast and at higher elevations in the centre of the island. Some plantation buildings had been tumbled by the force of the wind and falling trees, and a lot of chattel houses had been destroyed along the eastern coastline villages, including Martins Bay. A few people had been killed by flying objects.

His phone rang. It was Jessica.

"Are you up?" she demanded.

"Yeah." He frowned. "What's up?"

"Get dressed. I'll pick you up in fifteen minutes. Wear proper shoes."

Fifteen minutes later, the red car was pulling up to his building.

"Get in the back," she called out the window.

Dan opened the back door and climbed in. Stephen waved to him with a sheepish smile from the other back seat.

"Quickly," a male voice said from the front.

"John?" Dan said. "What's up, Jessica?"

"John will fill you in. I'm going to concentrate on driving through the debris."

John turned in his seat in the front and adjusted his glasses. "We're going to check on our mystery before the police do." He rubbed his hands together in delight. "A friend of my first cousin Agnes's neighbour passed on some news." He paused dramatically. "Two bodies were found in the boiling house of Coral Castle."

"What?"

"Actually, in the walls to be precise. The hurricane apparently blew off the roof, which landed far off in the yard of a second cousin to Agnes's neighbour."

"I really don't think we need all the genealogical details," Stephen said. Dan gave him a quizzical look so he added, "I'm here to support Jessica."

"Well that doesn't clear up anything," Dan muttered.

"The second cousin," John continued, unfazed, "went over to Coral Castle and found the skeletons. He didn't touch anything, but he knows we've been researching the Grahams and Coral Castle—"

"He does?" Dan asked in shock.

"This is a small island," John said waving away Dan's concern. "Everyone knows everything. And he thought we might like to investigate before the police are brought into this."

Jessica stepped hard on the gas and the little red car sped faster.

"Naturally, we think it's William and his wife," Jessica said. "Which would mean—"

"They definitely weren't killed in an accident," Dan finished.

"If Sean Mulroney killed them and put them in the wall, it would have had to be outside of sugar cane harvesting time, as they used the boiling house twenty-four seven. So that fits with his March fourth death. They didn't list her death."

"Wouldn't the slaves have suspected?"

"Wouldn't matter," Stephen said with a frown. "They had no power."

"Did the house survive?" Dan asked.

"They didn't say," John replied.

Jessica turned into the drive but they soon had to abandon the car. There were tree branches, vegetation, and a few whole trees strewn about. They stepped up their pace as they made their way to the higher elevation.

And finally, there it was. The coral house. It was still standing, though the winds had torn off some of the roofing shingles and a few shutters. The *for sale* sign was no longer in front.

"Did it sell?" Dan asked.

"I don't know," Jessica answered.

Despite the destruction from the winds, the monkeys were once again chittering up in the trees. They made their way around the windmill. It seemed to be no worse for wear, though some of the vegetation around it had blown clear. The boiling house was simply a few broken walls now. The group was quiet and solemn as they approached the wall, where they could clearly see two bleached white skeletons. Both adult sized. Their clothes were decayed over the years, but they looked of a grander design than a slave's.

"I always knew that God would show us the way," Jessica said quietly. "Maybe finally we will get to the bottom of all this."

"Maybe we won't," Dan said.

"But at least we can put them properly to rest."

As they got closer, they could see that the skulls were bashed in.

"Damn him," Stephen said softly.

"This is God's will, I am sure," Jessica said with conviction.

"At least they were together," Stephen said, putting his arm around her.

John was bending forward, studying the skeletons thoughtfully. "William was a tall man, wasn't he?" He murmured. "Could one man have lifted them alone?" He nodded his head in thought. "Someone must have helped him. Whether willing, or not."

He reached into his breast pocket and pulled out a penlight.

"Sheesh," Dan said, "are you always this prepared?"

"Yes, he is," Stephen said with a smirk.

John leaned over and shone his penlight into the portion of the wall that was still standing. "Aha."

They all leaned over to see. Another corpse was wedged into the wall.

"I assume on further investigation," he said, "they will find this is a slave.

"Something bad was done years ago here at Coral Castle," Jessica said shaking her head, "and God is finally revealing the sin."

***

They left when further investigation gave them no more insights. On the car ride back, they all agreed the search should move to the St. Cuthbert Treasures.

"I'll call Agnes," John said, "and tell her it's okay to send word to the second cousin to call the police."

"For our next step," Jessica said, "we need to try to find Hugh Montagu Junior and the Treasures. They might be separate mysteries, but I feel they're somehow related."

"And we can't forget little Joseph Graham," Dan said. Stephen looked at him with empathy. Dan shrugged. "He's gotten to me."

Stephen nodded. "That's how it is in Barbados. We're not that separate from the spirits around us."

"Well said, Stephen," Jessica said, smiling at him in the rear-view mirror.

"There's a book I purchased last year," John said. "It's about Christopher Codrington, so very serendipitous, in which the author describes the conquest of St. Kitts. Why not start with that for a little nighttime reading?"

After stopping at John's place to pick up the book, Jessica dropped Dan off. He went into his apartment, picked up his laptop, and went down to the Chefette restaurant next door. He sat at the outdoor patio, so absorbed in his reading he didn't notice the cars coming and going in the parking lot. For a couple of hours, he sat there, soaking up some sun, reading, and making notes. When he decided he'd had enough, after all, no one his age wanted heat stroke, he went back into his apartment. With his eyes still adjusting to the dark of the hallway, he went to put the key into the lock but found the door already slightly ajar. Remembering Silvia's hammer strike, he shifted his keys into his fist and quietly entered his apartment.

Everything looked almost untouched … almost. Things were just slightly off, as if someone had lightly ransacked his apartment. He held on tightly to his computer as he quietly moved from room to room, pulling back curtains, opening cupboard doors, holding his keys firmly in his fist, ready to use them at the slightest provocation.

When his phone went off, he jumped, "Ahh!" and then looked around, waiting for someone to charge at him. When it was apparent the apartment was empty, he answered the phone.

"What?" Dan said to his sister. His heart was still pounding in his throat.

"What kind of greeting is that?" she demanded.

"Someone ransacked my apartment." He continued looking around to see what they might have taken.

"What! Get out of there!"

"No, they're gone already."

"Did they take anything? Did they take your computer?"

"No, I had it with me over lunch," he said, looking over the desk in the living room, "but they got my flash drives. Damn."

He put down his laptop and searched through his paper notes, research from the Archives and the museum library. "They left my paper files, but they're in the wrong order."

"They probably photographed them. Do you want to stay at my place?" she asked.

"No," he said. "I appreciate the offer."

"I don't like this," Jessica said. "First you and Jack nearly get killed—"

"That was just bad drivers."

"How can you be sure?"

"Look," Dan said, "why would they want to kill us if they want to steal our research?"

"I don't know but—"

"Stop worrying. We just have to move faster." He went to the fridge and looked in. "Good. They didn't take my beer." He pulled one out and opened it. "So, why were you calling me in the first place?"

"We're all going to come over and help you research tomorrow."

"Who's we?"

"Me, John, and Stephen."

Dan grimaced. "I don't think that's a good idea."

"Well, I was going to ask if you were okay with it, but after this, I'm going to insist. We're safer in a group."

"Maybe that just makes us a bigger group of sitting ducks."

"Daniel Graham!"

"Jeez, don't call me that. Okay, okay. Just bring me more beer."

"I love you."

"Yeah, me too."

After he hung up, he decided to ask the building owner if he'd given the key to anyone. He found him cleaning the pool.

"Hey, Keith, did anyone go into my place today?"

Keith stopped and leaned on his pole. "Sure."

"Sure?"

"Yeah, you left that message about your sink today. But my maintenance man, Robbie, called in sick. Sent his friend in to fix it. Is it working okay?"

Dan frowned. "Oh, yeah, great. But I'd like to thank the guy. You got his number?"

Keith nodded. "You're a good guy, Dan. I don't have his number, but I'll get it from Robbie."

"Thanks."

"You recovered from that mad dog yet?" Keith called out.

Dan laughed and waved him off. "Mad dogs and Englishmen."

CHAPTER NINE
Relics and Rum

Dan opened his apartment door to invite in what seemed like a gaggle of people.

"Have you seen the newspaper?" Jessica said by way of greeting. She slapped the newspaper on the kitchen counter.

"Hi sis." It seemed too early for conversation. He had been up late into the night thinking about their puzzles.

"The police force are investigating the three skeletons found in the ruins of the boiling house at Coral Castle. They're bringing in experts from abroad to use up-to-date DNA techniques. I wonder if they'll ask us for samples."

John came in next with a stack of books. "Got lots to read today!"

Stephen followed him. "I come bearing gifts! Egg cutters and bakes!"

"Now, that's how to make an entrance," Dan said. He put on both coffee and tea, and the gang dove into the paper bags, helping themselves to breakfast. Cutters were popular any time of day. Egg cutters had fluffy eggs on fresh-baked crusty Bajan salt bread with lettuce and tomato and local pepper sauce. Bakes were a kind of fried dough. Dan loved the added cinnamon.

Once everyone had food and a drink, they settled down to investigate the books.

They started with a book on Durham to get a sense of where the St. Cuthbert mystery started.

"I've been to the city of Durham," Dan said, "many years ago. It's in Northern England." He pointed down to the picture of Durham Cathedral. It was in a book called *Durham Cathedral: The Shrine of St. Cuthbert*. "I was at a conference at Van Mildert College at Durham University and took a tour of Durham Cathedral. It's a World Heritage Site. It's supposed to be the greatest Norman building in England, perhaps even in Europe." He took another bite of his cutter. "I can't believe we're looking for something that was supposedly stolen from there." He shook his head. "Doesn't seem possible."

"I wouldn't have taken you for a religious man," John said delicately.

"Actually, I was intrigued by the name, Cuthbert, as our father's name was Cuthbert, which was shortened to Bertie by his friends."

"Could you blame him?" Jessica asked. "Imagine hearing Cuthbert all the time."

"He always said Cuthbert was an old English name of some English king."

"St. Cuthbert was born in 634," John said, "in Northumbria, a medieval Anglian kingdom in what is now northern England. He was a shepherd of sheep in the hill country on the Scottish border, before his religious career. He spent several years as a soldier before entering the monastery. He ended up retiring as a hermit."

"Look, John," Stephen said. "This Cuthbert fellow became a bishop in 685 AD."

"He was buried at Lindisfarne," John said as Jessica scribbled some notes, "but the community fled, and the monks moved his body and his relics in 793 to protect it from the Viking raids."

"That would be our fault, then," Dan said. Stephen looked at him quizzically. "We're part Viking." He lowered his voice. "You should know that about Jessica. Aggressive," he whispered with a wink. Jessica hit him with her pad of paper.

"They travelled around for years, finally settling in Durham in 995."

"Two hundred years carrying around a body?" Stephen asked in amazement.

Dan read from the book. "'Relics included monasterial door knockers, ancient seals, crosses, swords, silks, altars, ancient books and manuscripts, portraits, Bibles, rings, and ancient silver plates.' In 2012, the British Library acquired the St. Cuthbert Gospel. It's supposed to be the earliest intact European book and really well-preserved, a seventh-century manuscript." He paused for effect. "They paid nine million British pounds for it." The room was hushed.

Stephen swallowed his mouthful. "For a book?"

"I can now see why Angus Montagu is so keen to track down his ancestors' stolen artifacts," John said.

"Could that make him a dangerous man?" Jessica asked.

"Could do. Of course, we don't know what we're looking for exactly. Or what physical condition it's in. Maybe metals or precious stones would survive, but Barbados has a warm tropical climate, not like where the relics originated."

"The Battle of Dunbar, where our man, Montagu, was captured, was triggered by the death of Charles I and the Scots' recognition of Charles II as king, which the English rejected. So the Scots amassed an army of largely untrained young men, and Oliver Cromwell sent out seasoned professionals. The English attacked at dawn on September 3, 1650."

He took another bite of his cutter and chewed thoughtfully. "Apparently it was over in an hour. About 3,000 killed. About 5,000 captured and marched to Durham Cathedral, which was not being used. Thousands died of starvation or illness."

"And that's how our Montagu ends up at the cathedral," Jessica said.

"What's interesting," Dan said, "is that the treasures weren't supposed to be at Durham Cathedral when the Scots were imprisoned there. Around 1538, King Henry VIII dissolved the monasteries, destroyed St. Cuthbert's tomb, and took the monastery's wealth. The saint's body was exhumed, and apparently it hadn't decayed at all. They buried it under a plain stone slab."

He sat back visibly deflated. "The treasure wasn't at the cathedral at all. No way Hugh could steal it." He made a noise of disgust. "It really was all a fantasy."

The group was silent as they all digested this bit of news.

"What if . . ." Stephen started, "what if they hid some of it?" He flashed his eyes. "I mean, wouldn't you, if some damn king dissolved your monastery, destroyed your sacred tomb, and took your treasures? Wouldn't you hide some first? Just leave a couple pieces for them to snatch up?" They stared at him open-mouthed. Stephen shrugged. "That's what I'd do."

Jessica clapped her hands and whooped. "You're brilliant!" she said and pulled him in for a kiss. Stephen's cheeks turned a deep red.

John, seemingly unfazed by anything, took over the narrative. "It makes sense, as the Scottish soldiers treated the cathedral poorly. Montagu may have discovered the real treasures. So of the 3,000 prisoners who survived the march, minus 1,600 who died in the cramped cathedral from dysentery, we have about 1,400 transported as indentured labourers to English colonies in New England, Virginia, and the Caribbean."

"Hugh Montagu," Dan said, "welcome to Barbados."

"The indentured labourers were shipped out by November 1650, which is when Hugh Montagu would have been shipped to Barbados, so the timeline is right."

"John, regarding the theft of artifacts, it is said that even the English guards were stealing artifacts; one was accused of making off with the lectern. No doubt other items were stolen with the mass of prisoners in the open cathedral. So this is where the story of the prisoner Hugh Montagu stealing artifacts, may in fact be true."

"It would now seem that the descendants of those shipped to America in 1650 organized themselves into the Scots Prisoner of War Society," John said. "You should make a note of that, Jessica."

"Done." She added an exclamation point to her notes with a flourish.

"So the question is," Stephen said, "what could Montagu have stolen? It would have had to be small things, right? Like a ring or pieces of jewellery. Small enough to conceal in a small bag."

"Ooh," Jessica said, "the ring of St. Edward was lost during the dissolution."

John nodded, "Could be. Or something like that."

Dan rubbed his face. There was a lot of information running around. "So, we have Montagu at the Battle of Dunbar. He steals the artifacts of the St. Cuthbert Treasures and transports them with him to Barbados. He becomes an indentured servant to William Graham at Coral Castle and has a kid at age fifty with Maureen Yates."

Stephen looked at him blankly.

"That's from our research at the archives and museum," Dan said.

Jessica took over the story. "We know Hugh dies at fifty-nine and William becomes Hugh Junior's guardian. William gets married and has a son. I wish we knew the wife's name. But six years later someone bashes his head in and his wife's head in and seals them up in the boiling room wall. We suspect Sean Mulroney. He becomes legal guardian to Joseph. We know the boy dies young. His cousin Robert dies soon after William in mysterious circumstances."

"But what we don't know," John said, "is what happened to the stolen St. Cuthbert Treasures after Hugh Senior died. Did he tell William? Did Hugh tell his son?"

"No," Stephen said firmly. They all looked at him. "No one tells a kid that age about treasure or we'd all know about it." He gestured with his palms up. "Think about it. When you were nine, could you keep that secret?"

"You have a point," Dan said. He picked up his cutter again and finished it off, then reached over for some bakes.

"Hugh Senior might have told his wife, poor Maureen," Jessica said. "But if she was poor," she added, arguing with herself, "she would surely have sold it to make her life better. Maybe she would have taken back her child. I know I would have."

"If it was hidden somewhere in Coral Castle, maybe she couldn't get to it," Stephen said. "If she was poor and had a child out of wedlock, she was likely a lady of ill repute."

"I like how you said that," Jessica said. "Very old fashioned."

"You have a point, Stephen," John said. "She may have known about it but not been able to get it. One can only assume Sean Mulroney didn't know about it when he took over Coral Castle as he stayed there for another thirty-some-odd years, until 1736."

"But he went away 1732 the first time, when he shot a man," Dan said. "He came back four years later. That's when he was granted clemency and sold the plantation."

"I feel like we're spinning in circles," Jessica said, rubbing her forehead. "Hugh Junior or Sean Mulroney? Who got to them first?"

"Or are they still at Coral Castle?" Stephen asked.

For the moment, all they could do was nod.

"Well, we won't be able to get in there," Jessica said. "Not with all the police tape."

"Then we'll have to trace Hugh's steps and Sean's steps after they left Coral Castle," John said.

"You know what I'd like to do?" Dan asked, closing his laptop and standing up. "Go on a road trip."

"Anywhere in particular or just going stir crazy?"

"Well, during my failed date with Maria the other day, she mentioned a mixed race Montagu girl in her school. Maybe there are some descendants we can talk to. They might have some family stories. It's better than going stir crazy."

"A road trip sounds exciting," Jessica said.

Soon they were tidying up their breakfast things, hiding the books and laptop, and piling out the door. Once they were back in the little red car, their mood lightened considerably. It felt good to be actively doing something, where the only wheels spinning were the treads on the asphalt.

The roads had been mostly cleared of debris and the little car was soon speeding back along the path towards Coral Castle.

John was sitting in the passenger seat. He turned in his seat, book in hand and said, "From my sources in Poyer and Harlow—"

"Wait," Dan interrupted, "I thought we were doing a spontaneous road trip."

"He doesn't do spontaneity," Stephen whispered.

John looked at them over the top of his glasses as if they were recalcitrant school boys. "—I read that in 1689 the St. Kitts English garrison of 300 men held out against superior French forces for three weeks; however, they were compelled to surrender to the besieging French army of 3,000 men." He licked his finger and turned a page.

"The conquered English planters in St. Kitts were shipped off to Nevis, another English island nearby, which was swept by an epidemic of smallpox and fever."

"So, Hugh Montagu could have gone to Nevis," Jessica said.

"Perhaps," John relented. "Then with a series of strategic attacks," he continued, "the English forces attacked St. Kitts, and particularly with the gallantry of the Barbadian troops under Sir Timothy Thornhill, defeated the French. Thornhill himself was shot in the leg."

"So, he was likely still on the island," Jessica added.

John gave her a stony look. "Finally, a month later, that would be July, the French Army surrendered, the Union Jack was hoisted, and all the French citizens and soldiers were disarmed and shipped off to the French islands of Martinique, Guadeloupe and Marie-Galante—"

"So he could be—"

"My dear," John said with exasperation. "Can you not wait till I get this all out?"

Dan leaned forward in his seat. "No, she can't," he whispered.

"About 800 of the conquering English and Barbadian troops came down with wounds and fever."

"So Hugh could be dead," Jessica said sadly.

"Not before siring a son," Stephen said. "Angus Montagu, if in fact that's who he is, said he was the direct descendant."

"This doesn't get any easier, does it?" Jessica said, hitting the steering wheel in frustration. Then she said, "We're almost there. We're coming up to Coral Castle."

They waved to the plantation as they sped by. They could see yellow police tape across the driveway. The small village they were going to visit lay just beyond the plantation. Back in the old days, the slave houses would have sat close to the main house, looking similar to an old English village. Today they were driving to the parish of St. John.

Jessica slowed the car as they cruised down the street.

"What are we looking for?" she asked. "Are we just going to accost people on the street?"

"I'm thinking," Dan said. He was looking up and down the street when he saw two things that piqued his interest. The first thing was the Lemon Arbour, the best-rated rum shop in the parish of St. John, according to Peter Laurie's book *The Barbadian Rum Shop*. The second thing was Tarzan. *What is he doing here?*

"I think we should split up," Dan said. "Stephen, you come with me into the Lemon Arbour—"

"Yes!" Stephen crowed.

"—and John and Jessica, you go follow that man."

"No!" John complained as Jessica asked, "Which one?"

"The big hairy one who looks like Tarzan."

"I must protest—" John began.

"Sorry, John. Tarzan knows me—"

"So send Stephen—"

"—and you'll probably make the locals clam up."

With John still grumbling, Jessica parked and put on sunglasses, and they went their separate ways.

In Barbados, rum shops were equivalent to the local pubs in England; here, the males in the community would gather to chat and gossip, away from their women, and play games. Perhaps the activity taking place in a rum shop that truly captured the unique essence of Barbados was dominoes. In Barbados, it was an incredibly boisterous and noisy game.

Stephen and Dan went up to the bar and ordered a couple drinks. Then they casually struck up conversation with one of the shop patrons. Finally, Dan slipped in, "Hey, do you know if there's anyone called Montagu in the village?" He gestured to Stephen. "My friend Stephen here thinks he might be related."

"You'll want to talk to old Morris." He gestured to a wrinkled old man with very dark skin playing dominoes. "He's the oldest one here."

Dan and Stephen took their rum and sat near old Morris.

"Can we buy you a drink, sir?" Morris smiled and nodded. Once drinks were poured, Dan asked the question again about the Montagus.

"I heard ya, I heard ya," Morris said with a wide smile. "I may be wrinkled like dem prune but I can still hear! Montagu. Yes, there is." Morris took a sip of rum and let it slide smoothly down. "Dey is a family of mulattos who used to live in de village." He nodded. "I heard tell of dem long time ago. Dey done win the lott'ry or sometin' and move away to a high-White place. Tell de trut I en sure where. Maybe Amurca."

"Thank you, sir," Stephen said. "Please let me buy you all a round of drinks." He motioned to the barman.

"This is our lucky day," the barman said. "Two free rounds in one day."

Dan's head snapped up. "It wasn't by chance a Scottish man, was it?"

"No."

Relics and Rum

"Tall hairy man? Kind of like Tarzan?"

"No," the barman said as he wiped a glass. "He was a short Chinese man." He lifted an eyebrow. "I didn't notice if he was hairy."

Who the hell is that? Dan wondered. Trying not to frown, he turned back to Morris and added, "We're looking for another family as well. The Mulroneys."

At that, Morris lost his wide smile and his face shuttered. "Dey yer friends?"

"Not really."

"Keep it that way." Then he turned back to his dominos, muttering, "Dey have powerful bad blood."

Stephen and Dan could see they'd get no more out of Morris. Dan bought two bottles of rum for John and Jessica and tipped the barman, and they made their way back to the car where they were stopped short. Jessica and John were sitting on a bench chatting with Siggy as Tarzan stood mutely nearby.

"Dan!" Siggy said warmly.

"Siggy," Dan replied, "imagine … bumping into you here." Then he added in a bad Humphrey Bogart impression, "Of all the little rum joints in all the towns."

"Lame," Stephen muttered under his breath.

"Al and I were shopping. I got this beautiful little *treasure*"—there was an involuntary jerk from Dan's group as she said the word. She lifted her wrist to show everyone her new bracelet. "I do love gold and jewels. Al picked it out." Al grunted in acknowledgment. "And then we ran into your Jessica here, and I thought I knew her, but it must be her resemblance to you." She smiled and took Dan's hand in her own as Tarzan glared. "How is your trip going?"

"Great! Just great. Very relaxing." He held up his bottles of rum.

They all stood awkwardly for a moment before Stephen said, "We've really got to go. We got that thing. Nice to meet you, Siggy, Al," and he ushered his group into the car.

"He saw us," Jessica said in a low voice as she put the car into drive.

"I think the term is 'he made us,'" John corrected.

"That's because … " and they bickered between themselves as Jessica stepped on the gas. They were finally placated when Dan showed them his gifts for them and began filling them in on what they'd discovered.

"An Asian man too?" Jessica asked. "How many people are looking into this?"

"Enough to make me believe it's all true," Dan answered.

"Well, we may never find out what happened to Hugh Montagu," John declared. "I think our best bet is to follow Sean Mulroney's trail. Dan," he added as he looked fondly at his new bottle of rum, "fancy a trip to the Carolinas?"

CHAPTER TEN
Charleston, SC

The young man knocked at the door of the derelict wooden house.

An old voice croaked, "Come in." The old woman sat in a rocking chair in the corner of the room by the window.

"Grand-mère Maureen," the young man said.

"Who are you?" she demanded. "You look rich."

He laughed and straightened his coat. "I have done well in the family business," he said.

She beckoned him closer, pulled him down, and squinted. "Hugh?" she gasped.

"No, Grand-mère, he is dead. I am his son, Phillippe."

"Are you a planter?" she asked.

"Phff," he mocked and then leaned in to whisper, "I am a pirate."

She nodded. "Like your grandfather," she said. "He once told me about his treasure."

Dan had never been to South Carolina, but John had gone there and bought a book about it. It was sitting in his carry-on bag and promised some fascinating if dry reading.

It hadn't taken long to wind up things in Barbados and purchase a new ticket. He'd called and left a message at the Sandy Lane Resort, telling Maria how sorry he was to cancel the swim date but he'd been called away on business. For one wild moment, he thought about inviting her along, thought about marching into the resort, grabbing her, kissing her, and making her see she would be his Antoinette forever. In fact, he had it all planned out. She could try to sell Barbados real estate to the South Carolinians. Play up their mutual past. And if it turned into a torrid romance, well, what her mother didn't know wouldn't hurt her. But, the moment passed, and instead he left his polite message.

Then it was hugs all around with his family and friends at the airport.

"You promise me you'll be safe," Jessica demanded, crying. "I will never forgive myself if something happens to you."

"Relax," Dan said. "I'm just going to be researching. The worst I'll get is a paper cut."

But when Stephen shook his hand, he said softly, "Be safe, man. There's some bad folks moving around."

That's when John gave him the book to read. He gave them a final wave and went through the gate to airport security.

He'd be about six hours in the air, stopping first in Miami and switching planes to Charleston. Silvia had booked him into a boutique hotel, the Meeting Street Inn, near the South Carolina Archives, the home of the South Carolina Historical and Genealogical Society, in the Fireproof Building on Meeting Street. In 1827, when the archive building was completed, it was considered the most fire-resistant building of its day.

He had to wait a long time for a cab as a man with dreadlocks scooped the one he was getting into. Dan cursed as he waved to another Charleston Cab. The cab finally pulled up in front of a tall narrow, vividly pink-stucco building with a long white verandah. It was a "single house," with a narrow façade on the street side and a large piazza.

Each room opened up to the central courtyard. It was built in 1874, had once housed a saloon, and was walking distance of the old historic market.

He went through the arched doorway and into the lobby to check in. Jazz was playing over the intercom and a chandelier sparkled overhead. Everywhere the furniture was ornate and period. He opened the door of his room to find a four-poster "rice" bed with carved rice stalks on the post and a lacy canopy overhead. He imagined Maria would have loved it. She was a woman after all.

They could have had breakfast together, and then gotten to know each other a little better ... while he had the energy. He suddenly felt very tired. He thought he'd just relax for a bit before starting up his research. Dan flopped onto his stomach on the white quilted comforter just for a minute. To rest his eyes.

In his mind he was back in the Bajan sea and Antoinette was wearing a little red thong number. She jiggled up and down slightly as the waves brushed up against her. She was smiling in a sultry fashion, her tongue slowly moving across her bottom lip.

"Dan," she whispered, but he could hear it across the waves, feel it across his skin.

"I'm coming, Antoinette." He walked towards her in the water as she frolicked like a mermaid, the sun glistening on her body. But the farther he walked, the farther she seemed to be.

"Dan," she called in her siren voice, "come to me." He wanted her so badly he began to tremble. He felt as if his whole body was vibrating and water was splashing on his face. "Dan, *Dan* ..."

He woke suddenly, feeling the vibration of the phone in his pocket and aware that his face was lying in a puddle of his own drool. So much for romance.

"Hello," he croaked into the phone.

"You made it alive!"

"Jessica?"

"I just wanted to make sure you made it safely. John wants a few words about your next move—" He could hear the phone being jostled. He closed his eyes again.

"Dan, this is John."

"I know," he mumbled.

"Wake up. You need to look for the Mulroney plantation, Grahamfield, and take some photos. That is, if it's still there. But take photos even if it's just the grounds. But first, go to the South Carolina Historical and Genealogical Society Archives, 100 Meeting Street. See if you can come up with anything we don't already have. Look for family references, big purchases, whatever they've got. We need some evidence he had the treasure with him. Did you ever visit Arlington in Speightstown, Barbados?

It is very similar to the Barbadian houses in Charleston. It will give you a feel for Mulroney—remember the Barbadian settlers to Carolina left from Speightstown in the 1670s."

"Mulroney," Dan mumbled.

"You need to think like the bastard to find him."

"Hmmm, bastard."

"Dan, are you listening to me? Are you even awake?" John's voice moved away from the phone. "I think he's asleep."

"Asleep," Dan murmured.

"Dan?" Jessica's laughing voice was back on the phone. "Get some sleep, little brother."

"Mmm." And with that, Dan dropped the phone and his mind went back to the warm Bajan sea.

***

Dan left the hotel the next morning feeling refreshed and ready to get to work. He thought he'd soak up the culture and get a feel for the town that Sean Mulroney called home by taking a walking tour. He downloaded a historic Charleston self-guided tour at *Free Tours by Foot* and plugged in his earbuds.

The tour started at the Old Exchange and Provost Building. It was massive, stately building that had been built in 1767 and used as a dungeon during the American Revolution. Sean Mulroney wouldn't have seen it when he first came in 1736.

The Old Slave Mart on Chalmers Street would have a few ghosts, Dan assumed. The arched entryway made Dan think of an open mouth. It was built way outside his time period; in 1859 when public slave sales were prohibited, the trade moved inside to a private location.

Next was the Pink House on Chalmers Street. Dan stopped to get a good look at it. It was very pink. It was built of pinkish Bermuda stone in the French Quarter around 1712 as a tavern with a brothel upstairs. It looked decadent. Apparently Chalmers Alley was part of a rollicking business that serviced the wharfs nearby. To Dan, it looked like some of the old Bajan houses in Bridgetown. He could imagine Mulroney visiting the women. As he turned to continue down the sidewalk, he bumped shoulders with someone.

"Sorry," Dan said. "Such interesting architecture."

He heard a muttered, "Tourist," and turned to see a man with a hat pulled low striding quickly away.

Dan thought he saw a dreadlock peeking out from under the hat. *Him!* Dan wanted to shout, "Hey buddy!" but didn't have time for a fight.

With a huff, he moved to the next place of interest. It was an ornate building on Church Street, with an intricate wrought-iron balcony. It was built as a hotel around 1809, The Planter's Hotel, Charleston's last surviving hotel from the antebellum period. At that time the hotel's guests were mainly planters from around the state, who came to Charleston for the horse-racing season. Maybe this was where the Goose Creek planters from Barbados sojourned in the hot Carolina summer season.

He passed St. Michael's Episcopal Church on Broad Street, with its tall tower clock, and Coates' Row, a cluster of brick and stone on Bay Street, which housed a tavern in the 1600s where thirsty sailors visited while in port.

These buildings look a lot like those old late seventeenth-century buildings in Bridgetown in Barbados, Dan thought.

He stopped for lunch at Hyman's Seafood Restaurant back on Meeting Street. He settled down at a table and snacked on boiled peanuts while he waited for his Charleston lump crab cake sandwich. He jotted down a few notes about what he knew and what he needed to know.

He knew that Mulroney had come to Carolina on the barquentine *Endeavour* in 1736, but that's as far as the trail led. He wanted to see if any other Mulroneys or Montagus showed up in the records, especially if their location suggested they might be of mixed race. Had Mulroney brought anyone with him from Barbados? What did he need to know? He could feel the weight of time; it was running out.

Once he finished the last bite of crab cake and slaw and hushpuppies, he paid the bill and pushed away from the table. It was time to track down Mulroney.

The Fireproof Building was a square and powerful building set by itself on a corner. Its heavy, fluted columns and large triangular pediment atop the columns made it look like a Greek temple. Dan had a good feeling about it. Surely the information he needed was well secured in this building.

He went inside. It was large but interesting, with alcoves, winding stairs, and ironwork. He found a place where he could set himself up to check the records.

Dan set out a new pad of paper and a few of his favourite uni-ball gel pens. He quickly discovered the name Mulroney in the immigration records and his deed for the Ricefield plantation in Goose Creek. But below this listing, there was a Montagu—Nathaniel Montagu. He was head of a free mulatto family from Barbados, who settled in South Carolina in the Lowcountry. Dan made a note of it and then looked in the wills, births, and burial data, but he doubted that this family had anything to do with stolen treasure; they looked pretty poor.

It wasn't long before he found Sean Mulroney. A lot of Sean Mulroneys. His lawyer, it seems, died not long after he bought Ricefield and renamed it Grahamfield. He died in 1738 at aged fifty-nine. He had a son, who died in 1745 at age thirty-four; he must have been born in Barbados in 1711. He had a son, Sean, when he was twenty-six, who had a son, Sean, when he was twenty. It started getting confusing and Dan didn't know if he was happy they were all named the same so he could find them more easily or justified in cursing them all for making this so hard. Soon his tidy white pad was a scribbling of names and dates and arrows and stars.

Mulroney had two daughters, Hannah and Elizabeth, and another son, Thomas, but Dan didn't focus on them as the eldest son would have inherited the plantation under the English law that ruled South Carolina, and time was tight.

He found the will for Sean Mulroney, the crooked lawyer, (as he was starting to think of him, *Sean-Mulroney-the-crooked-lawyer*) but it seemed straightforward with an inventory of the plantation. He found the will of both the son and grandson but then nothing after the American Revolutionary War of 1776.

"This is not helpful, Sean," he said in frustration. He pulled out his phone and dialled John's number.

"You've found something," John said, "or you're stuck."

"Stuck. Look, John, I'm in the archives and I found Sean Mulroney, a lot of them. They seem to be popping up and dying off every few years. I found the plantation he bought after he arrived. Then he died about a year later, and after the American Revolution, there's nothing. I feel like it's a dead end."

"Well," John said in an annoyingly calm voice, "it looks like your man was probably a Tory and on the wrong side in the revolution. He, one of your Seans, probably had his house confiscated. He could have fled south to the Bahamas or Bermuda, or north to Upper Canada. He may have got killed in the Revolution. Is there any burial record in South Carolina?"

"Well, there are lots of burial records. I got to write this all down again and try to figure out if anyone came out alive. What's wrong with naming your kid Harry or Jeffrey?"

"I'll search the censuses for Bahamas and Bermuda," John said. "That's as far as the Loyalists got. They would have lost everything and had no money, so it may be they were attracted to free land in Canada. We'll need to check the Canadian records for United Empire Loyalists." He added, "Did you find any wills?"

"Yeah, for three generations, but it's just standard stuff, no treasure." He started listing off the house and land, slaves and contents of the house, "including furniture, ceramics, tea canister."

"Tea canister," John said. "Is it in the other wills?"

Dan shuffled through his papers. "No. In the son's will, there's a tea chest. Let's see … the grandson's will says 'tea caddy.'" He frowned. "They can't all love tea that much, can they?"

"No," John said, his voice rising in excitement. "No, they can't. But they can love treasure that much. You see what this means—Sean Mulroney is our man, forget about the brown Montagus."

"It exists," Dan said in an awed voice.

"It exists," John agreed.

There was silence as they each absorbed the moment.

"I'll call Jessica and Stephen. You see what else you can find. And, Dan," John said, "this is real now. Watch your back."

Relics of a Saint: A Barbados Mystery

Dan walked back down Meeting Street, seeing nothing but the past. He had read up more on the action in South Carolina in the War of Independence to get a better feel for the Sean Mulroneys.

South Carolina had vacillated between the forces of independence and loyalty. Even though independence was declared in Charleston in 1776, the town fell to the British in 1780 until Britain was finally defeated in Yorktown, Virginia, in 1781. In January of the next year, the South Carolina Whig government, which urgently needed money, called for the confiscation of property of all those individuals who had aided the British.

In the end, 4,200 White loyalists from South Carolina who could not live in an independent America had immigrated to the British Caribbean, East Florida, England, and Canada. The 1790 South Carolina census showed a Nathaniel Montagu, but no Sean Mulroneys. Dan figured the St. Cuthbert Treasures would have left with Sean.

For a moment he almost felt sorry for the Mulroneys. To have lost everything because you were on the wrong side of a war. He needed to go to Goose Creek to satisfy his curiosity. He wanted to walk on the same ground as the Sean Mulroneys.

He realized he'd walked past his hotel and turned back abruptly almost running over a young woman quickly exiting a building.

"I'm so sorry—" he said grabbing her arm to steady her and looking into her face. "Maria!"

"Dan," she smiled broadly. "Surprise!"

"What are you doing here?" he asked. "I mean, I'm glad you're here. Just … surprised … you know where I am." He frowned until she leaned in to give him a kiss.

"But you told me, remember?" she laughed and gave him a hug. "When you left your message."

"Did I?"

"Of course," she said confidently. "You said you had to fly away to Charleston on business. I too have some business I can do here." She smiled suggestively and Dan was warmly reminded of the Antoinette swimming in his dream. "So I thought I'd mix business with pleasure."

"Do you want to spend the day rolling around in the hay?" Maria asked.

"Damn right," said Dan nearly swallowing his tongue, and his heart went into overdrive. Sean Mulroney went clear out of his mind.

"Do you have some business to carry out first?" she asked, so he put his arms around and pulled her into a kiss. Her lips were soft and pliant, but she pulled away. "No," she said. "I mean, real business."

"Oh," he said, his libido deflating, "I was thinking of renting a car and driving out to Goose Creek to see an old plantation."

Maria clapped her hands in delight. "Oh, a road trip!" She wrapped her arm in his. "Maybe," she murmured leaning her breast against his arm, "we can find a little out-of-the-way motel when we get there."

They walked back to Dan's hotel, arm in arm, quickly organized a rental car, and were soon on the road driving north towards Goose Creek along Highway 26.

The creek was a tributary of the Cooper River in the Lowcountry. Before the first White settlers came, the area was populated by the Etiwan tribe of the Wassamasaw Indian Nation. They seemed to be on friendly terms with the first English settlers to Berkeley County—Barbadians of English descent who settled in Goose Creek area and formed a powerful political faction known as the Goose Creek Men.

Goose Creek was a swampy area, and many of the early plantations were built on bluffs with water access. Barbadians, mainly staunch Anglicans, settled there first. Later, other groups like the French Huguenots arrived, but the Goose Creek Men kept control of politics.

Back in that day, South Carolina was an unhealthier place than Barbados. It had malaria, yellow fever, and in 1738 and 1760, a smallpox epidemic. Growing rice in water was bad for one's health, and as a result the average age of death of the early White planters was very young; half the Anglican Church ministers that went there died within ten years. It was also miserably hot in summer. This led many of the planters to be absentee owners and go to Charleston, close to the ocean to keep cool.

The slaves from Africa were more accustomed to the climate and the work—West Africa was already growing rice—and they were healthier. In Goose Creek alone, in 1708, there were 2,787 people in total, and of those, 2,333 were Black slaves—eighty-four percent of the population, which helped South Carolina become such a wealthy colony. And before the American Revolution, everything produced could be sold in the British Empire.

The decision to leave the British Empire would have been a complicated one for the White plantation owners; they depended on British markets but they could identify with Northern protests against increased British taxation.

Dan turned onto Highway 17.

"Keep an eye out for an archaeological dig sign. Grahamfield is nearby." Another old plantation nearby had been the subject of an archeological dig in 1987 and there was renewed interest in the old ruins, which had become tourist attractions.

"There!" Maria exclaimed and Dan turned into a long bumpy driveway through a forest. Unlike the old plantations in Barbados, there were forests and the forests were unkempt. As they went along, they saw through the trees the derelict shells of several outbuildings. As they approached the end of the driveway, they saw what must have once been a magnificent two-storey brick house. There was a big earthquake in 1886, which left it only a shell of itself.

They pulled up to the ruin and got out.

According to the records, at Grahamfield, Mulroney grew indigo, rice, and corn. He had seventy-one head of cattle, fifteen oxen, and sixty-five slaves, and was worth about 4,000 British pounds. He would have spared no expense on his house.

They walked carefully around the house. There were remnants of a wide circular staircase up to a wide centre hall. Old stone showed where a grand fireplace once was.

Dan was finding Goose Creek a kind of dismal, depressing swamp country. It was obviously much hotter in summer, with no trade winds as in Barbados to cool you down. Despite the shade, he was dripping sweat. He could understand why the planters would spend the summers in Charleston near the sea coast.

"I'm happy I grew up in Barbados, instead of Goose Creek," Dan said. "In Barbados I could swim every day of the year, in the warm Caribbean sea. It was walking distance from my house." He looked around at the massive piece of land, imagining all the bad things Sean Mulroney did to get this. "I'd rather be poor in Barbados, than rich in Goose Creek," he murmured.

"You seem sad," Maria said. "I know what will make you better."

She put Dan's hands on her voluptuous hips and started moving them sensuously. Then she leaned in and, it was like heat erupting, they were kissing passionately.

"Oh, Dan," she moaned as he thrust his pelvis towards her. "Oh, Dan." Then she was crying, "Dan!" and he realized by her tone it wasn't from passion. He dragged himself out of his passion and turned around.

A black SUV had driven up the driveway and parked on an angle, barring their way. Two men got out. They were both wearing dark-tinted sunglasses. One man had no hair; the other was wearing dreadlocks.

"You!" Dan said, fear and fury battling in his chest. He pushed Maria behind him.

The bald man pulled out a switchblade. Maria gasped. He walked towards Dan's rental car and slashed a tire.

"What are you doing!" Dan demanded.

"It's either the tires ... or you," He said in slightly accented English. Dan was too scared to place it. The man calmly proceeded to slash the other three tires.

The man with the dreadlocks said, "Give us your cell phone or you're a dead man."

When Dan didn't move—his fear and anger had made him effectively immobile—the man came towards him and threw a punch. It slammed into Dan's jaw, but instead of frightening him, it seemed to motivate him. He flew at the man and soon they were punching and grappling and beating each other. Dan really thought he could eventually take him, until he heard Maria scream. He looked up and saw the bald man holding Maria with his knife pointed at her throat.

Dan got up and so did the man with the dreadlocks. The man reached out his hand; his eyes said, *Don't push me*, so Dan reached into his pocket and pulled out his cell phone and wallet. "Your keys, phone and wallet," the man said. Dan gave him the wallet and cell phone but stepped away and threw the keys into the forest. The man punched him hard in the face and snarled, "Rasshole." The bald man reached into Maria's bra—"you pig!"—pulled out her phone, and then pushed her towards Dan.

Just then a tour bus arrived and the two men, ran into their SUV and left, Dan could only watch them stunned. *Rasshole* was Barbadian slang for "idiot." This was no random theft. This had to do with the treasure.

Dan walked off into the trees.

"Dan, what are you doing?" Maria called out. He bent over in the grass and groaned. "Are you going to be sick?" she asked.

"Looking for my damn keys." He walked along bent over, straining his eyes. "Seemed a good idea at the time," he muttered. "I was trying to save myself a hundred bucks to replace them."

Maria followed him into the foliage and gave him a hug. "You are a good man, Dan Graham." Then she pulled away from him. "But you look like hell."

He looked down at himself. His pants were dirty and ripped. There was blood on his shirt. And he could feel his face swelling. One eye wasn't quite working right and his body was screaming … everywhere.

"I've had better days," he said.

"Ah!" she cried. She reached down and raised her arm in victory, shaking the keys in her hand.

They went to the car, cleared out their stuff and then walked—Dan limped as the tour bus drove up

***

The tour bus pulled over ahead of them and the door opened with a metallic screech. As Dan and Maria walked towards the door, dozens of interested faces looked out through the window.

"You folks need a lift?" called the bus driver. He had an older friendly face and a ball cap. "My name's Ronnie," he said.

The people on the bus were all atwitter at Dan's bedraggled state. Someone snapped a picture with a flash. The words "mugged" and "tires slashed" and "phones stolen" were guaranteed to make them instant celebrities. People bunched up together to give them prime seats at the front of the bus. Dan insisted he didn't want to call the police—he didn't want to slow down his search because of red tape. Anyway, he knew the men would be out-of-towners. Meanwhile, the bus driver called the car rental company to pick up the car and said he would take them back to Charleston.

"You're so kind," Maria said.

"Thank you very much," Dan said.

"Just got to finish up the rest of the tour, right folks?" the bus driver said in a cheery tone and pulled out his mike. "Now on your right, you'll see …"

Dan leaned back in his chair, closed his eyes, and tried to tune it all out. He thought about the Barbadians, as he now thought of them. They could now search his emails, the websites he'd visited, photos he'd taken, documents he'd stored there. With his eyes closed, he touched his swollen mouth and ran his tongue over his teeth. It felt like all his teeth were still there. Maria gave his hand a light squeeze.

"What you might not know," Dan heard Ronnie saying, "is that pirates were pretty common down here in Carolina back in the day. And they weren't all like Blackbeard, all crazy-eyed and smoking beards. Some married our women, bought some land, and settled down. For years we welcomed them at port even after the British banned them. But after a while, we got tired of them, oh about 1715, and that wasn't a good thing if you were a pirate.

"Look what happened to the famous gentleman pirate, Stede Bonnet. He was an educated, cultured, wealthy sugar planter, who took off one night with his crew in a ship he built, leaving his wife and kids behind in Barbados, and raided all the ships trading between Barbados and Charleston. They say it was his nagging wife that drove him to it. Who here would leave their naggin' wife for a life of piracy?" A bunch of hands raised in the air as the women screamed with laughter. "How 'bout you, ladies, would you leave your husbands?" Almost all the women raised their hands. "Whether we should blame his wife or not, Bonnet was hanged in Charleston after a lucrative career of pirating. He was found guilty and hanged on December 10, 1718.

"But most of the pirates didn't come from a privileged life. Many had been indentured servants. Rather than working in the hot sun on some Barbados sugar plantation, they grabbed the nearest boat and ran off to become a pirate. Certainly better than cutting sugarcane in the hot sun. Slaves too. And army men. Why, they could be treated badly on a navy boat." Dan opened his eyes and slowly turned his head to focus on Ronnie.

"It was a way for indentured folks to get back at the English, who had treated them so badly. Ever heard of Captain Blood? He was an indentured servant in Barbados and had been a qualified medical doctor and surgeon in Devon during the Monmouth Rebellion in 1685; imagine that, a qualified medical doctor and surgeon. That's skilled stuff. He was an Irishman who'd been captured by the king's troops when he was treating a wounded rebel during the battle. He was arrested, sentenced to hard labour, and indentured for seven years in Barbados."

"He escaped and, determined to make England pay, became a famous pirate. Scourge of the Royal Navy. There was even a Hollywood movie, starring Errol Flynn."

"Oh, I saw that," a woman said, and the conversation degenerated into an argument about who had played the best pirate on film.

"Pirates," Dan said thoughtfully.

"Just like what happened to us," Maria said, snuggling into him.

"Pirates."

CHAPTER ELEVEN
Follow the Trail

Phillippe watched his quarry climb out of his coach and head towards a tavern. He had followed Sean Mulroney from his mansion.

All day he had seen Black slaves visibly shrink in the man's presence. Phillippe spit on the ground. He'd heard of slave treatment from some of his crew. He had a business proposition for Mulroney. He followed him into the tavern.

Three hours later, they emerged and shook hands as partners.

"Alors, I will call tomorrow and we will begin the search?" Phillippe asked.

The punch to the side of his head came out of nowhere and, disoriented, he stumbled back.

"I think I can search myself," Sean said smiling as he beat the man to death. Then, he pulled out his gun and shot him, just because it felt good.

"Calm down," Dan said into his new phone. He was sitting in the waiting area in the airport.

"Calm down!" Jessica's voice shrieked. "I won't calm down. You were attacked! You could have been killed."

"I didn't do that badly," Dan said.

"This is no laughing matter!"

"Look," Dan said trying to take back control of the conversation, "the treasure isn't here; I just know it. I've got a flight to Toronto, leaving tonight at 7:34. I'm flying American Airlines to Charlotte, and then Charlotte to Toronto. I should get in around midnight. So, I'll be offline from about six-ish. Don't freak out."

"Don't freak out?" Jessica demanded. "When did this happen?"

"Two days ago," he mumbled.

"Two days ago!" and she was off on another rant about siblings and social contracts.

It'd taken him that long to deal with the car, his credit cards, and money; find a new phone; and buy an airline ticket. Not to mention sending off Maria. He was in no physical state or mental state to have a torrid affair. Mostly he was just sore. His face was still swollen. And he hadn't slept well. The first night he dreamt someone was breaking into his room. He woke up trapped in his bedclothes, kicking and shouting. And last night, he woke up to the sound of a child crying under his bed. No, the sooner he got out of Charleston, the better. He was cracking up. He'd packed up and taken a cab to the airport hours before he needed to.

"Oh, I have a theory I want you to run by John," he said. "Maybe he can use his superior research skills to track something down."

"What did you find?"

"I didn't really find anything; it's just because of what Ronnie said."

"Who's Ronnie?"

"The tour bus driver— Anyway, he was talking about pirates. Did you know indentured servants, slaves, and *navy men* sometimes joined pirate crews? What if Hugh Montagu, Junior joined the pirates after the Battle of St. Kitts?"

There was silence on the other end of the line.

Dan said uncomfortably, "Well, I know it's a long shot—"

"It's brilliant!"

"Good," Dan said smiling into the phone. "Good. While I'm waiting for my flight, I'm going to be searching the land records of the United Empire Loyalists Association. See if I can find any land grants or lot numbers. Can you see if you can find anything about pirates or Montagus in the pirate areas?"

Follow the Trail

He opened up his laptop, plugged it into an outlet to keep it charged, and started searching. As the hours ticked by, he discovered that the main waves of Loyalists to what is now Canada happened in 1783 and 1784. Nova Scotia and New Brunswick got 30,000; Ontario got 7,500, who settled along the St. Lawrence; and Quebec got about 2,000. Cape Breton and Prince Edward Island were created to deal with the influx. Even free Blacks and escaped slaves, who fought in the Loyalist corps, as well as 2,000 Indigenous Iroquois allies from New York State, settled in Canada. The Loyalists were offered free land in Canada, and some of the Loyalists from the South brought their slaves with them; it was still legal in Canada.

To get the land, you had to submit a written petition with other documents to the British government. Dan had a good feeling he was close to the end of this mystery. The petitions had to include the applicant's story about their service, losses, and suffering during the American Revolution. If you could prove you remained loyal to the British Crown and were persecuted and forced from your home, the British government would help you.

In the records he located a Sean Mulroney who had settled in the Township of Blenheim, Chatham-Kent, Upper Canada. His status was "Proven," but that was it. No lot number, no other information. Dan would have to go to Chatham-Kent to get more details if he wanted to poke around, get the lay of the land, and maybe channel Sean Mulroney. That thought brought an involuntary shiver.

He got on the plane when his flight was called, and the rest of his travel was overshadowed by his research. He went through all his notes to see what he'd missed, the pirate Montagu always foremost in his mind. Did he retire an old man or die by a sword or a musket ball? He must have had a family. Where did he leave them? If he was a pirate wouldn't he have come back to get the treasure? Did he know about it? Around and around his mind spun. How and when did Sean Mulroney take the treasure? All these pirates stealing something that was sacred and holy. Dan shook his head and finally fell asleep.

He spent the night at the airport hotel, the Canadian hotel staff being too polite to ask about his face. In the morning, he rented a car, said a silent prayer that all would be well, and began his trip to Chatham. He started his journey on the massive Highway 401. He changed lanes often and kept checking his rear-view mirror to shake off any pursuers, and then he suddenly cut onto a rural highway. He stayed on it for a while and then got back onto the 401 till he hit Kitchener. This went on throughout the trip: switching roads, changing lanes, checking mirrors, hands tight on the steering wheel.

His first stop would be the Chatham Land Registry Office; it was a small low-rise building behind a spacious front lawn. He was getting pretty used to the drill. Inside the registry, he gave the lady at the desk the name Mulroney.

"Wow," she said. "You're the second person in as many days to do a search on his title deeds. Are you a descendant as well?"

"That's— that's amazing," Dan said. "Not family," he said, recovering. "I'm writing a book on the Mulroney family. They were originally from Barbados, you see. They immigrated to South Carolina and then, being Loyalists, moved to Upper Canada."

"That's so interesting," she said.

"Can I ask, was it a Scottish man?"

"A Scotsman."

"Oh, really," Dan said.

"No," said the woman, wrinkling her nose, "I was just correcting you." Her fingers were flying across a computer keyboard, multitasking as she spoke. "The man," she said, pausing to read a sentence she was writing, "was Asian." Dan's head popped up. *That Asian man again—*. "Barbados is a lovely place," she said. "Are you from Barbados?"

"Yes, I was born there. I just came back from a trip there."

"What a coincidence. One of our librarians just came back from there too. Let me call her." She pulled out her phone and quickly texted a message. "She'll be right out." And around the corner walked—

"Siggy!"

"Dan?"

"What are you doing here?" they asked at the same time and then leaned in for a hug.

"I guess you two must know each other," the woman said a bit sourly.

"Candace, we met on the plane to Barbados," said Siggy.

126

"Is Tarzan still around or is he working out in front of a mirror, keeping those pecs and abs toned?"

"You're so funny, Dan. That's what I like about you."

"It's because I'm Bajan born. We're great dancers, love music, and are great in bed; when the music stops the rhythms keep vibrating through our bodies. No need for a vibrator, when you have a Bajan man in the house."

Siggy laughed and asked, "Is that a pick-up line? I sure think growing up in that hot weather must be great for the libido. Better than growing up in a cold place like Norway."

"It's the bikinis men see all year-round in Barbados, keeps our testosterone levels high and heats up the environment, but in my experience," he added with a meaningful look, "I've found Norwegians can be very exciting too. At least the women are. I have no experience with the men, but high testosterone levels can be bad for prostate cancer."

"There you go again," Siggy said, "making me laugh, I am sure that you won't get cancer."

Dan let it slide; it would be too complicated to explain. He suddenly remembered Candace and slid a glance her way. Her mouth was open as if she was scandalized.

"I thought you were staying longer in Barbados," he said to Siggy.

"Nope. Time was up. So what brings you here, Dan?" Siggy asked. "You're looking up"—she leaned over to look at Candace's notes—"Sean Mulroney. Is this part of your family mystery?"

"You could say that. Any plans to come out to British Columbia to visit your relatives? Maybe without Tarzan? I have had bad experience in the past with Norwegian girls in a confined area, like a bedroom, with a Tarzan hanging around."

She slapped his arm. "You're too bad. But no, no plans."

"You should come out and stay at the Coast Bastion on Vancouver Island. The beds are comfortable, and I know a great seafood place that serves Fanny Bay oysters. It's good for the libido." Dan looked over at Candace again; she shut her mouth with a snap and looked back at her computer.

"Would you like me to help you with your search?" Siggy asked.

With her assistance, Dan discovered that Mr. Sean Mulroney, like many Loyalists, got 200 acres and started a tobacco farm in Blenheim, near Dresden. He also found a son, Sean, who was born in 1787 and died in 1848. In this Sean Mulroney's will, he found a reference to a tea caddy. Dresden was interesting as that was where the Black ex-slave Loyalists had settled along with the Africville settlement in Nova Scotia. It seems these were the only places in Canada that Black people had settled in those days. Later some settled on the Gulf Islands off the British Columbia coast in the 1860s he thought.

"Yes!" he said.

"What's made you so excited," she asked.

"It's—" he began, but something in the gleam of her eyes stopped him. He studied her a moment. "You don't have any Scottish blood in you, do you?"

"Me, Scottish?" She laughed. "I love your humour."

He discovered the farm was sold in 1865, and there were no further records of a Sean Mulroney in the Chatham area. The trail had gone cold again.

He pulled out his phone and dialled John in Barbados. "Hey John."

"My favourite wayward man," John said heartily. "Are you calling with good news or questions?" Dan moved off to the side and lowered his voice.

"Questions and suppositions. The trail runs cold in 1865. The farm is sold and there are no more records."

"Given there was no plague in Canada in 1865," John said, "I think we can rule out death. Canada became a country in 1867, so maybe there are some clues there. Logically, just as they got land for free in 1784, perhaps they moved to another part of Canada that was opening up at that time, as they seem to be adventurers by nature.

"Manitoba and British Columbia opened up at that date. Since these were Barbadian descendants via South Carolina, my educated guess would be British Columbia. Prairie winters can be a tad cold. Buy yourself a plane ticket, my boy. You're going home."

Dan tucked his phone back in his pocket. "Well, it's time for me to go."

"Be back tomorrow?"

"No, for good," he said. "It's time to go back home."

He pulled her to him and kissed her softly on the lips. For once she wasn't laughing at him.

"*Ha det*," he said.

"You know how to say good bye in Norwegian."

She touched her hands to his still-swollen face.

"*Hold deg trygg*, Dan. Stay safe."

CHAPTER TWELVE
Moody v. Douglas

"So you're back," Henry said as Dan strolled into the tennis club, a racquet in hand. "How was it?"

Dan pulled a few tennis balls out of his pockets, ready to serve. He was feeling out of sorts. He'd been back for two days and was already feeling down. That's when he called Henry to play some tennis and sweat a bit. Henry was always able to get him out of a funk.

"Great," Dan said. "I nearly got killed twice, saved a woman's life, almost had passionate sex with a variety of women, survived a hurricane, got my tires slashed, was nearly mauled by a dog, and I thought I saw a ghost. You know, same old, same old."

"That would explain the face."

"It was quite an adventure, and it's not over yet." As they hit some balls back and forth, Dan told his story in fits and starts.

"And now," he said, smacking the ball across the net with frustration, "the trail's gone cold again."

"How about I buy you a nice cold Canadian beer?" Henry asked, throwing his tennis towel across his sweaty shoulders. "Let's go to Joe Fortes."

Over lobster rolls and beer, Dan talked about Barbados. He couldn't help thinking about it with regret. As much as he loved West Vancouver, his boyhood home was calling him more than ever. It must be the damn mystery.

"Did you know Joe Fortes's dad was from Barbados?" Henry asked, looking over at the photos of Joe Fortes on the wall. They showed Joe's portly figure in an old-fashioned swimsuit of 1920s vintage with a striped top and also in a three-piece suit with a prominent gold watch, hanging out his fob pocket.

"And some say Joe was from Barbados too," he continued, "though Trinidad claims he's theirs. Nice to have people fight over you. Joe was the first lifeguard for English Bay Beach.." Joe had a library, school, and restaurant named after him in Vancouver, where Dan used to eat lunch occasionally. Dan remembered that the restaurant had pictures of Joe on the wall. Dan wished that he could have met Joe, gone over and shook his hand, and thanked him for being such a great representative of Barbados. Dan could imagine all the obstacles that Joe would have had to face in those days as a lone Black man in a racist white society.

Joe Fortes was a bartender on a British ship that came to Vancouver in the late nineteenth century. He settled in a little beach cottage on English Bay Beach in Vancouver. The beach reminded him of Barbados. Joe had worked as a bartender in Vancouver's Gastown and patrolled English Bay as the lifeguard. He taught many of the Vancouver upper class how to swim and saved over a hundred lives. When he died in 1922, he had the largest funeral ever recorded in the history of Vancouver up to that point.

"Barbados connections seem to be popping up everywhere," Dan said as he took another bite of lobster roll. "You're a realtor," he said. "Do you know anything about the history of that connection? Something you might sell to prospective buyers? I would dearly like to not have to look at more microfilm."

Henry chuckled and speared a crisp French fry off his plate. "Well, you're in luck, my friend. It's one of my nerd proclivities. Let's see, race, the Caribbean, in-fighting. Where to start? Another beer might help."

"I'm buying," Dan insisted.

Henry took a long drink of his new beer and began. "You may know that Sir James Douglas, the first lieutenant governor of BC was born in British Guyana to a Scottish planter, his dad, and a free Barbadian "mulatto", his mom. He apprenticed to the North West Company in his teens, and then the Hudson's Bay Company when they merged in 1821. He married the Métis daughter of the Hudson Bay's chief factor, so both Douglas and his wife were mixed race. Douglas had a great career: the Bay's chief factor, built Fort Victoria, and in 1858 he became governor of Vancouver Island.

By 1864 we had the Gold Rush and it was crazy in Victoria, especially with Americans flooding in and people thinking they'd take over. During his tenure as governor, it was said that because of his mixed race parentage, and mixed race wife, he was very generous with groups that were always subject to racial discrimination; he welcomed immigrants regardless of ethnic background."

"He allowed Blacks like Mifflin Gibbs the first black person elected to public office in Canada in 1866, from California to settle in large numbers on the islands off Vancouver Island, the Gulf Islands and also Polynesians from Hawaii. He treated the native Indians with justice and fairness. He allowed Jews to own property and run for public office, with Victoria having the first Jewish mayor in the history of North America, in 1865."

"The rest of BC, called the colony of British Columbia, had its own lieutenant governor, Richard Clement Moody; that's where you get the name Port Moody. Like you said, lots of connections. His family were upper-class English, who owned a lot of properties in the Caribbean. Moody was born at the British military complex at the Garrison in Barbados. He was commander of the Royal Engineers and the first lieutenant-governor of British Columbia in 1858. They say he fathered at least two illegitimate children with his Indigenous housekeeper.

"So obviously some class and racial differences between the two men. And when Vancouver Island was amalgamated with the colony of British Columbia to become the Province of British Columbia, we had problems. The men hated each other, their jurisdictions overlapped, and they were constantly feuding. Moody had higher prestige but less authority than Douglas. Moody had nothing but scorn for Douglas."

Dan took in this information in silence. "So, if you were Sean Mulroney," he finally said, "would you be attracted to Douglas's Victoria or Moody's BC?"

Henry toyed with his glass as he thought about it. "Hmm. An interesting dilemma. He was not the plantation owner till he stole it through murder and deceit. Would it give him a chip on his shoulder towards the upper crust?"

Dan thought about Sean Mulroney constantly trying to find a way to have the upper hand. Why? Maybe he wanted to be rich enough and powerful enough to be respected. But, those kind never did get respect. He would have hated Moody too.

"Victoria," he said decisively. "My gut tells me Victoria. When I get to the city, I'll hit the books again."

He insisted on paying for lunch. "You're a gold mine, Henry. The least I can do is feed you."

"Just let me know how it goes!" Henry said. "And good luck."

Feeling much better about the mystery and even life in general, Dan headed back to home. When he got to Victoria, he'd look up the Victoria Genealogical Society and search in their pioneers index. They were getting closer. He could feel it. They were in the 1800s; that was almost the twentieth century. He wanted to find a real live Sean Mulroney. Make him see where he came from. Make him say sorry. *Then, take his treasure and run*, he thought with a grin.

At home, he packed a small bag for a few days, sifted through his notes again, and then sat down with some Barbadian rum to call his sister.

"Hey, Jessica," Dan said into the phone. "I've got a good feeling about this."

"About what, little brother?" she laughed. "You sound better than the last call."

"I think I found him. I'm tracking him to Victoria."

"Well, don't go just yet."

"Why's that—" but he was cut off by the sound of his doorbell.

"'Cause you have guests—"

Holding the phone tightly, Dan went and gingerly opened the door.

"Uncle Dan!" Silvia came rushing in, followed by Jack and Stephen, who was loaded with luggage.

"Jessica!" Dan said into the phone.

"Call you back," she said and ended the call.

"Silvia, Jack, Stephen," Dan said weakly, shutting the door behind them. "Why?"

His niece gave him a dark look, pulled out her phone, and snapped a photo of him. "Mom said you'd act this way. She doesn't want you by yourself, so you're stuck with us. If you don't want me to send her this photo of you right now, you won't put up a fuss, Leo wanted to come too but Mum said he was too young."

"You mean your little brother, blonde Leo with the bright-blue eyes? You're blackmailing me," Dan said, aghast, as Stephen muscled by him to take the luggage to the living room.

"Yes," she said matter-of-factly and swiped her phone to look at his photo. "You look like hell by the way."

"I like the purple edges," Jack said. "You look cool. Like you're a spy or something."

Stephen added as he came back into the room, "With those bruises, maybe not a great spy."

Dan walked into the living room and grabbed his small bag off the couch. "Okay," he said, "you can come with me. I think I've tracked Sean Mulroney to Victoria."

"Let's not be too hasty," Stephen said. "We set out tomorrow—"

"What Stephen's trying to say," Silvia cut in, "is that he wants to eat dinner at the Red Lion pub in West Vancouver—"

"It's a British-style pub with a wooden antique British bar on the main road in Dundarave," Jack added, "a little village of shops, close to the ocean—"

"A favourite spot of West Vancouverites especially those from England, 'cause it serves Yorkshire pudding once a week. And today's—"

"—the day!" Jack finished.

"We heard about it the whole trip," Silvia said. "If you don't drive us all there, Stephen will likely explode."

***

Named for Queen Victoria, the city of Victoria was one of the oldest on the Pacific West Coast. It was filled with colour from gardens big and small around the city and surrounding neighbourhoods. It was a mix of British architecture and habits, and Indigenous arts and culture.

While the kids took Stephen souvenir shopping on Government Street, Dan hit the Victoria Genealogical Society. Lo and behold, his guess was right; he hit pay dirt again—he found a Robert Sean Mulroney living in

Victoria in 1866, and the law firm of Mulroney Mulligan. There it was, in black and white for all to see, Sean Mulroney, another Mulroney lawyer. He took a photo of it and texted it to Silvia. She sent back a photo of Stephen hugging a life-size stuffed bear dressed like a Mountie.

He was able to trace the birth of a Sean Mulroney in Victoria in 1866, and the death of one in 1926. If they were keeping up the naming tradition, except for the rebel who named Robert Sean, perhaps they had passed on the treasure. There was a gap of a generation..

If they moved, where to? Maybe a bigger city like Vancouver for better business opportunities. Or the Gulf Islands or Okanagan Valley for retirement. They could have moved up the east coast of the island to a little seaside retirement town like Qualicum Beach or Fanny Bay.

With these questions in his mind, he headed downtown to meet his group of protectors. *Not protecting too much when they're running around like tourists*, he thought with irritation. He was meeting them in the Bard and Banker, a bank built in 1885 that had been converted to a pub, with winding staircases, huge chandeliers, and a long, well-polished bar.

His protectors were already seated and waving him over. They had a table across from the huge TV, their souvenir gift bags clustered around them. They were each wearing a new hat creation from Roberta's Hats. Silvia was wearing a beret; Jack, a pork pie hat; and Stephen, a fisherman's cap. "Look what we got you!" Silvia called, holding aloft a fedora. She fit it on Dan's head as he sat down. "We got Mom a stormy rain hat in purple. She'll love it."

"So did you have any luck?" Stephen asked, handing him a menu.

Dan shook his head. "Yes and no. I tracked them to 1926, then we lose them for a generation, and then we get too many Mulroneys. It'll be like finding a needle in a haystack. They could be in town. They could have gone anywhere."

"Have some food," Silvia said. "It'll all look better."

They placed their orders—Humboldt squid, two Bard burgers, a mussel pot, and a cold beer all around. As they ate their lunch, described their touristy morning, and considered their next steps, the news came on the TV.

"Ooh, someone's died," Jack said. Since the sound was off, he pulled out his phone and found the news station. He turned it on so they could watch on the big screen but hear the sound.

"—were killed in a boating accident off the coast of Gabriola Island. The RCMP say the couple had no children and they are looking for kin to notify. The couple drowned while scuba diving off the Gabriola Caves. The RCMP think they may have been swept out by one of the dangerous riptides that sometimes occurs near the Gabriola Caves and drowned. While they wouldn't tell us their name, we spoke to someone who was a neighbour." The clip switched to an old man and what looked like his wife, sitting awkwardly on their couch.

"They were nice people, but kept to themselves. Seemed to like to hike around the island a lot, looking for hidden Spanish treasure he used to say," the man said.

"They must have explored every inch of the island," the wife said. "But I can't imagine why they were scuba diving! He had a heart condition, and she wasn't a good swimmer. And after they had that break-in just last week."

"Makes you wonder what's wrong with the world," her husband added.

"This reporter has discovered the couple's names were Sean and Leanne Mulroney."—everyone around the restaurant table gasped and Jack turned up the volume—"Long-time members of the Gabriola Island community, Sean was a lawyer and Leanne worked for the local newspaper, the *Gabriola Sounder*."

"Wasn't his dad a lawyer, too?" the woman asked her husband. "Frank here used to laugh, and I know that's a terrible thing. If only we'd known they would die so horribly. But he did wonder if they weren't an uncreative family—"

"—because they were both named Sean too."

Dan stood up and waved for the server, "Check please!" Everyone around the table started scrambling to grab their bags. "We've got to get to Gabriola as fast as we can," Dan said. "Everyone else is going to know too."

***

Gabriola Island, was one of the Gulf Islands off the east coast of Vancouver Island in the Strait of Georgia. To get to Gabriola Island, they had to drive "up island" to Nanaimo and then take a small ferry over to Gabriola. Dan drove with his foot slammed on the gas the whole way, considerably shortening the two-hour trip. Soon they were lining up and then driving onto the ferry.

"Okay, everybody," Stephen said, grabbing their attention as they were getting out of the car, "hats on and sunglasses. If Angus or the other unknown treasure seekers are around, we don't want them recognizing us."

"Thank goodness for Roberta and her hats," Silvia said. With her beret, dark sunglasses, and a scarf, she looked like a movie star.

They went up on the open top deck to enjoy the wind and sunshine, and explore all the views of the Gulf Islands passing by, just like any other tourist. Behind their dark glasses, they were assessing everyone onboard.

They passed cute little red-roofed houses, and on one little island was a lighthouse. Stephen cried out in awe as a pod of orcas swam by. He snapped a picture "for Jessica." Overhead, seagulls flew on air currents, and Jack thought he saw an eagle and a blue heron.

Gabriola had been formed out of sedimentary rock from the ocean floor that was later scoured by glaciers; the waves that battered it over time sculpted amazing shapes and caves. There were also natural and artificial reefs that made for great diving adventures. It had been the home of the Snuneymuxw, a First Nation of the Coast Salish people, for thousands of years. More than seventy petroglyph rock carvings could be found on the island.

Explorers also came to the area, sailing up the North American west coast from Mexico and California. The Spanish started coming in 1700; Captain George Vancouver found the island in 1783. Many of the islands off the BC coast were given Spanish names, like Gabriola, Cortes, and Valdes. There was also the Strait of Juan de Fuca.

Settlers came in 1874, building small farms where people kept sheep and grew fruits and vegetables. They'd sell their produce at small roadside stands using the honour system: a suggested price, a money jar, and no one in attendance. You could buy eggs and even cuts of meat in roadside refrigerators. The people on Gabriola were environmentally conscious.

"Jack, have you identified where that couple Frank and his wife live, yet?" Dan asked, pulling them back to their task at hand.

"Why were they out scuba diving with a heart condition and bad swimming skills?" Stephen asked. "They had to be on to some treasure. That wouldn't be recreation for them. Seems odd for the treasure to have been hidden in the Gabriola Caves, though, doesn't it? Seems risky."

"We're going to need some diving equipment," Dan said.

"When was the last time you went diving?" Stephen asked, his voice laced with skepticism.

"Too long ago," Dan said, "but I've been sent two professionals." He pointed towards Silvia and Jack, who were standing off to the side, taking silly selfies. "Well, they're able bodies anyway."

They loaded back into the car, rented a motel room and headed to a dive shop to pick up gear. When they told the shopkeeper what they wanted, she said, "That sure is a popular activity today. You're my third set of customers today asking to go diving in the caves." As she gathered the equipment she added, "You want to be careful though. Don't want you getting in trouble like the Mulroneys."

"I know, it's just devastating," Silvia said. The others looked at her with narrowed eyes. What was she up to? "I sure hope Frank and …"

"Terry."

"—Terry are okay. My mom is worried about them."

"Oh, does she know them?"

"Yes, she was in that group with Terry, the, um…"

"Quilter's club—"

"Yes, that's just the one. I'd love to stop by and have a chat with her, send my mom's love, but, you know I don't even have their address." She dropped her expression. "It's all so very sad."

"Oh, aren't you sweet," the woman said, and soon she was directing her how to get to their house.

As they left with their gear, wet suits, maps, and an address on a slip of paper; Dan couldn't help looking over at Silvia with respect.

They decided Stephen would man the boat they'd rent while Jessica and Jack went diving. Meanwhile Dan was going to try to break into the Mulroneys' house and see if he could tell what they'd been up to.

Their next stop was the marina to rent a speedboat. Once again they heard they were last in line.

"Oh," Dan said casually to the man renting them the boat. "Was that my friend Scotty? Well, that's what we all call him in the dart league," he laughed heartily, "that's because he's Scottish. A Scotsman named Angus Montagu?"

"Close but no cigar." The man continued getting their order ready. Then he suddenly said, "It's Monty Eu, not Montagu. Are you sure he's a friend of yours?"

Dan's eyes widened. "Yeah, my … Asian friend."

"Well, probably Eurasian or mixed," the man said. "You really shouldn't be so closeminded."

"Yeah, you're right. Thank you so much for your help. We'll take good care of your boat."

As Stephen took off in the boat with Jessica and Jack, Dan drove out to the address on Berry Point Road. There were houses along the water. He found the house that belonged to the older couple. It was very tidy but not ostentatious. The Mulroney house either had to be the house on the right of the older couple, or the house on the left. He looked to the right. The house looked tired but lived in, with a riot of mismatched flowers and plants in the front yard, and gnomes, lots of gnomes peeking out of the bushes. Quirky. The house on the other side was tall and handsome, made of rich wood and glass. It spoke of wealth, not warmth. Bingo. He drove a short way beyond the house, then got out of the car and ran back through the bushes.

All looked quiet. The house looked sealed up tight.

Dan moved through the bushes to the back of the house. There was a balcony off the second floor with a sliding glass door. He'd snuck through those kinds of doors before in his youth, trying to visit girlfriends. He was pretty confident he could get in again.

He looked around for something to climb on. There were a couple of garbage cans. He placed one garbage can on top of the other and climbed up. For a moment he thought all was well, but then the bottom can collapsed. As he swayed precariously, he lunged for the balcony and caught the railing.

He was hanging there, feeling his shoulders separating from his arms, realizing it looked much easier on TV. He tried flinging his foot up so he could catch the railing. Once, twice, on the third try, when he was sure he would topple to the ground head-first, his foot caught the railing, and he slid his legs over the balcony, his body following with a thud. So much for being a spy.

He struggled to his feet and pulled on the balcony door, expecting it to be locked tight. But it slid smoothly open. Dan stepped into Sean Mulroney's house.

CHAPTER THIRTEEN
Miracle

The woman knocked on the door of the mansion and asked the Black slave if she could see the master of the house. He showed her to a room to wait. When the master walked into the front parlour, he spied a beautiful mulatto woman dressed in a flowered mantua.

"Why do I have this pleasure?" Sean asked.

"I am searching for my husband," she said.

"I've been away for four years," he said dismissively, "I know nothing of your problem."

She hissed, "You killed him in the street."

"I was attacked by a pirate," he sneered. "I killed him in self-defence."

"I will expose you!"

He hit her across the face and punched her. When he was done, he pulled out a bag of money and threw it at her. She spit at him from cracked and bleeding lips.

"You will take this money and leave Barbados," he said,

Weeping, she took the money and left the room.

He poured himself some rum and sat down to quench his thirst.

"I will tear this place down if I have to, but the treasure will be mine."

After all the time spent with his head in the past, Dan was surprised to see the furnishings upscale but modern. It was kind of a disappointment. He realized that in his mind he felt he would somehow come face to face with an evil Sean Mulroney, who had murdered his family, beat his slaves, and killed them if he needed to or wanted to. He was someone with so much rage he could beat a man to death, then get it excused, because of the status he stole from a dead man, woman, and child. But all Dan saw around him from a Sean Mulroney descendant was simplicity and taste, from the framed artwork to the beige-toned quilt on the bed, to the over-stuffed leather chair by a stained glass lamp.

He hated to think he might have liked this Sean Mulroney.

He carried on out of the bedroom, down the hall, and down the stairs, looking in the open doorways till he found the office.

Inside the office, the air felt stale. He looked around for the computer, but couldn't find it. No computer. No laptop. No tablets. But there was a printer. Someone must have taken the computer. He went over to the bookcase to check out the books. Lots of books on treasure. Pirate treasure. Spanish treasure. He pulled one book out after another. This guy was seriously obsessed. But it was the wrong treasure. What about St. Cuthbert's Treasure? There were no books on Durham Cathedral or anything of the past. Nothing except for pirates. Only one pirate came to mind: Hugh Montagu, Junior. Could there be a connection?

Between two books he saw a tiny piece of white. He pulled it free. It was an ad ... for metal detectors:

"Are you looking to uncover deeply buried treasure caches? Deep-seeking metal detectors are specially designed to locate hidden treasure. Large volumes of gold and silver coins, jewellery, and other precious metals are often deeply buried beneath the earth in large vessels. While treasure comes in a wide variety in shapes and sizes, with the proper equipment they can be easily located. Visit us at—" The rest of the ad was ripped off. He turned it over. There were some letters and numbers written on the back: MGCP WLHL 5BHL 4FW.

He kept staring at the letters, hoping they would make some sense. He decided to look for the metal detector in the house. Maybe it was tucked away somewhere. He made a methodical search under every bed and in every closet. When he got to the kitchen, he passed the calendar, held on the fridge with magnets, and reflexively looked at it. There was a circle around the fifteenth of the previous week and a note scrawled on that day: *Malaspina Galleries Community Park*. It took a moment before his brain made the connection. MGCP. He looked at the paper. Could the treasures be hidden in the caves? Was he this close? He opened the broom closet next to the fridge, calmly, almost as if he knew he would see it. Standing up among the brooms and mop was a metal detector. He grabbed it and a shopping bag hanging on the back of the door.

Then he heard something that made him freeze: the sound of the balcony door upstairs sliding open on its track. He wasn't alone. His heart pounding in his ears, he quietly opened a few cupboard doors till he found some large plastic containers. Then he opened one of the drawers and took out a few large serving spoons. As he heard soft footsteps moving down the hall, he crept to the front door, pulled it open, and ran.

***

Dan was back in his car, speeding down the road toward the caves. The torn piece of paper was in his sock in his shoe and the treasure books he'd swiped, under the seat. Suddenly, a car swerved around him, and cut him off, nearly plowing into him. It was a black SUV.

He swerved out of the way and drove onto the shoulder of the road. This time, he wasn't backing down; time was of the essence. He jerked on the steering wheel and his car slammed into the SUV, forcing it off at an angle. Dan looked over to see a startled face in the window.

"Siggy!" he shouted. "What are you doing!"

The car came back towards him and he got a glimpse of the driver. Tarzan. Of course. Trust that over-sized, hairy man to be an aggressive driver. Both cars swerved again. Suddenly, Tarzan swerved his car into Dan's car with a metallic crunch. Dan returned the favour, turning his wheel into Tarzan's car. This time, they were pushing each other, the metal dented and buckled between them, the force keeping both of them straight. Suddenly a car was speeding towards them head on. Dan could see the fear in the driver's face; the man waved his hand frantically. At the last moment, Dan swerved the other way and went driving up onto the embankment, fighting the wheel so he didn't flip over. The SUV went hurtling into the bushes.

"Yes!" Dan said as he got back on the road. He would reach the caves first. He parked the car with a jerk, grabbed the metal detector, stuffed the spoons and containers into the shopping bag, and ran. His mind wanted him to unwind the mystery of how Siggy and Tarzan were connected to the mystery, but *there was no time!*

He ran through the small parking lot and tore down a path along the water and out onto a narrow promontory with a little cove on each side. Then he stepped down onto a rock path that formed a shelf along the edge of the sea. Light-brown-coloured rock hung over top, carved out by eons of ocean waves.

There were strange circular holes in the rock face, the ground rock, and the roof. It was called the galleries. Dan passed large oblong pools in the rock, where seawater had collected as the tide came in.

He picked his way more slowly, though he felt the pressure of the need for speed. He passed signs that read Overhanging Cliffs Use Caution, and Danger No Entry. He had no intention of skidding and falling to his death. Some of the arbutus trees on the edge of the cliffs above the caves looked precarious, their soil eroding, as if they were about to fall into the ocean because of eroding soil.

He was getting closer to the spot the Mulroneys had died.

"Uncle Dan!"

He squinted his eyes against the glare off the water and saw Silvia standing in the boat waving to him.

"Get down!" he shouted. He sprinted the last hundred yards and ran down the very edge of the water, waving their boat in. He had to stop himself diving into the water and swimming towards them. These were no warm Caribbean waters. The hypothermic temperatures of the Pacific Ocean could kill you.

When they got close enough, he waded out towards them, threw the metal detector and bag into the boat, climbed in, and said, "Go, go, go!"

Stephen, bless him, asked no questions, just revved the engine and sped away. He found a secluded area and killed the motor.

"I was in the house, Sean Mulroney's house, and it wasn't what I expected …" He told them in a jumbled way about what happened when he went in the house. " … and then I found this!"—he brandished the metal detector—"and this." He carefully pulled out the piece of paper and turned it over. "There's a clue," he said solemnly showing it. "MGCP WLHL 5BHL 4FW."

"I didn't know what it was at first, but then I saw handwriting on their calendar on the fifteenth."

"That's the day they croaked," Jack said.

"Exactly," Dan nodded. "And on the calendar was written Malaspina Galleries Community Park."

"MGCP," Stephen said with excitement, his eyes flashing.

"We need to figure out the rest," Dan said.

"Let Silvs take a look at it," Jack said. "She's really good at puzzles."

Silvia looked with surprise at her brother. He gave a lopsided smile and shrugged.

Dan handed her the paper, but when she looked at it, nothing immediate came to mind. "Let me think about it for a while. We need to go back into the water and try out your metal detector. Maybe we don't need those clues."

Stephen started up the motor and explained where they were going to dive. "We've already looked for the first round. It's pretty shallow, so that helps. There are also rocks and crevices that could really anchor something."

"The metal detector is just what we need," Jack said. "There wasn't much visibility."

"We want to look around the mouths of the caves," Stephen added. "We can set the boat off a little bit."

"I want to go down this time as well," Dan said. "Just in case there's trouble."

He suited up and soon he was giving a thumbs up and entering the water with Silvia and Jack. They swam calmly and steadily, making sure they stayed well in sight of each other. Jack held the metal detector. Dan held the shopping bag.

They swam to the seabed just around the caves. Jack gave a thumbs up and pointed. This was where Mulroney and his wife had died. Dan handed the metal detector to Jack. He wanted to be free to keep a look out and periodically look over his shoulder.

While they were being slow and methodical, they knew they had limited air. Suddenly, the metal detector flashed light, and even under water, they heard a distinct beep. Jack pointed. It was a spot where someone had already cleared out the rocks. *This must be it!* Perhaps the Mulroneys had simply run out of air in their desire to get to the treasure.

As they got farther down, they started digging. They dug and dug, Dan checking over his shoulder, checking his watch. He felt sure something terrible would happen to them. About two feet down, someone's spoon hit something hard. Excitement building, they began clearing faster, trying to find the edge. It seemed too big for a tea chest. It looked more like a trunk, the size of a small suitcase. Breathing heavily from the effort, using up more oxygen than they should, they finally cleared enough to get around the trunk. They dug beneath it so they could use leverage to make it move. It was too heavy to lift straight up. They'd have to somehow drag it to shore.

They worked together to move it to the shore and hid themselves under an overhanging arbutus tree. They pulled off their mouthpieces and heaved in fresh air. While Dan and Silvia stayed with the trunk, Jack climbed up to the edge of the water and scrambled away to find Stephen. Dan and Silvia stayed partially submerged in the water, shivering, from cold or adrenaline, being as quiet as possible.

After a few minutes they heard footsteps on the path above them. Silvia was about to call out, but Dan held his finger to his lips.

"Where'd you say you saw them?" Dan heard a distinctly Scottish voice say. He flashed his eyes at Silvia and she made no sound. That had to be Angus.

"I thought it was here." It sounded like Tarzan.

"Let's go back this way again and be more methodical." Dan was sure that was Siggy. His heart sank.

"We're running out of time," Angus said. "We've got this close. Let's finish it."

They listened to the footsteps move away and all was quiet again. Just in time, as they heard the sound of a motor and Stephen and Jack came zooming into sight.

Together they hoisted the trunk into the boat and climbed in. The boat was now sitting low in the water. Then everyone but Jack laid down in the boat. They figured Angus, Tarzan, and Siggy knew the rest of them by sight. Jack started the engine and moved forward in an even, moderate pace. They didn't want to attract any unwanted attention.

They hadn't gone far when Jack whispered, "That's them!" But he carried on looking around in a nonchalant fashion, as if he were a regular tourist. He even smiled and waved at the trio. Once they were obviously clear of them, he veered towards the shore so Dan could leap out. He was going to make his way back to the car while the rest of them headed back to the marina. He'd drive there so they could load up the car. It worked like a charm. Soon he was parking the car at the marina.

He grabbed a shopping cart he saw leaning derelict in the bushes and pulled a black garbage bag from the trunk of his car.

As he quickly wheeled the wobbly shopping cart towards the water Silvia came running up to him.

"Great idea, Uncle Dan."

Together, they loaded the trunk into the garbage bag, lifted it into the shopping cart, and guided it back to the car. Only once they had it in the trunk did they take a breath of relief.

"We have to open this now," Stephen said. "Is everyone thinking what I'm thinking?"

Silvia nodded her head. "Yeah—"

"—that's no tea caddy," Jack finished.

Silvia picked up one of the chisels out of the toolbox Dan kept in his car. Then she handed it to Dan. "Here, Uncle Dan. You have to do this."

He fit the tool into the lock and pushed until it broke. He pulled it off carefully and said, "Together."

They all grabbed the lid, lifted, and gasped. Spanish gold. After standing and simply gaping, they finally looked around to see if anyone was nearby.

"Shut the lid," Silvia hissed.

They shut the lid, laid everything in the back of the car, bags and sweaters and a tarp on top, closed the car trunk, and piled into the car.

"Let's stay in a different room tonight," Dan said.

When they finally made it back to the motel and quietly changed rooms under Jack's name, they sat in the living room around the treasure chest, speculating on what they had. Dan now got Jessica and John, from Barbados, on the speaker phone.

John, researching Gabriola, figured the naval captain Dionisio Alcalá Galiano and his crew had buried it under the caves for their own benefit, intending to return. But one year later, in 1792, Captain George Vancouver arrived on the scene and the Spanish could no longer access it.

"But what about the St. Cuthbert Treasures?" Jessica asked. "Are we giving up on it? Isn't that what we're really looking for?"

"We're at a dead end," Dan said with frustration, pulling at his hair. "I've destroyed two cars looking for it."

"Don't forget we have the clue," Silvia said. She pulled out the clue and sat studying it. "MGCP WLHL 5BHL 4FW." She started thinking aloud. "We know the MGCP stands for Malaspina Galleries Community Park. John, we think it was hidden recently because someone burglarized Sean Mulroney's house. So, it has to be somewhere accessible, but not so accessible a tourist could find it."

As the group carried on talking, making plans about what to do with the Spanish treasure, Silvia played with the clues. She tried switching the letters around to make words. "Maybe it's like a text short form with no vowels." She started trying out different vowels in different spots till suddenly she shouted, "Wall hole!" She got excited. "Wall hole five bee hole four fuh wuh." She frowned in disgust. "Well that doesn't make sense."

"Maybe only some of it's a no-vowel word," Jack said, sitting on the arm of her chair to look at the clue. "I mean, the Malaspina clue was an acronym."

Silvia nodded. "You have your moments, Jack. Five B. Five back. Five before. Five bottom—"

"That's it," Jack said. "Malaspina Galleries Community Park, wall hole five bottom hole, four … feet west."

Miracle

The room went silent. Jack looked up. "That's it. That's it!" he shouted. He jumped up and grabbed his sister's hands and they galloped around the room laughing.

Once they'd all settled down, they started making plans. Their biggest worry would be how to conduct a physical search of the Gabriola Caves, in such a public area when it was full of people swarming over the area and diving off the rocks.

"We can go tonight," Jack proposed.

"No way!" Silvia said. "That's a great way of killing yourself. Didn't you say there were signs all over the place about falling rocks and dangerous places?"

"That's it," Dan said. "We can go dressed as workmen—"

"Work persons," Silvia corrected.

"The caves recently had some areas designated as dangerous areas. Some of those overhangs looked like they could fall any moment."

"We can take a few bags," Stephen said. "Maybe split up the relics in case there's trouble."

"Good thinking," Silvia said.

"Jack should get us the work clothes," Silvia said, "and hats and stuff. Can we wear face masks because of dust?"

"More good thinking," Jessica crowed on the speakerphone. "Let's wind this up. John and I will sign off." Then she added, "Please, everyone, stay safe."

Early the next morning, Jack went out in search of their disguises. He even found a wig for Stephen. It wasn't strictly necessary, but it sure lightened the mood when he put it on.

Once they were dressed in their work persons' overalls, they hid the gold in various places in the motel room and asked to have no maid service. Then they loaded up into the car. No one spoke. They were all tense and expecting danger.

They borrowed a car from a motel staff member, paying way more than they would have at a car rental place, and drove to the Gabriola Caves. Acting as though they were meant to be there, they began counting the wall holes.

"Here's the fifth one," Silvia hissed. She stood there casually while the others counted off four feet west. They found a deep hole set high up. There was a lot of debris in front of it, so it could be easily missed. It was too high for any one person to reach.

"You'll have to climb on my shoulders, Silvia," Stephen said. "You're the lightest."

She climbed on top of his shoulders and carefully stood up. She reached up and cleared away the debris carefully.

"I expect at any moment a snake or rat's going to bite my hand," she laughed nervously, "like in the *Indiana Jones* movies." She stuck her hand in and … nothing happened. "No snakes," she called down. She stretched out and reached further in, until she was in up to her shoulder. When she pulled out her arm, she was holding a cylindrical shape covered in burlap.

"Bingo," she said softly. Something struck the rock near her head and pieces of chipped rock flew off, cutting her face. They heard the shot after the fact. Stephen pulled her with him to the ground. Another shot rang out.

Dan grabbed the bundle, hoping they'd stop targeting Silvia, stuffed it in his knapsack, and urged everyone to "Get the hell out of here!"

They moved back along the track, crouched over. They were heading towards their car when another shot rang out ahead of them.

"Into the trees," Dan called out.

When they got deep enough into the woods, they leaned over to breathe and clutch their sides.

"Should we call 9-1-1?" Silvia asked.

"Then we'd have to explain about the treasure box," Dan said, "and we don't even know what's in it exactly."

"Oh, I think we know," said a voice as a gun cocked. They looked up and froze. Angus was close by in the trees. Tarzan had a gun cocked, aiming at Silvia.

"Give me the bag, Dan," Angus said, "and no one gets hurt."

Dan took a step forward and started reaching for the bag to give it to Angus when Silvia ducked, leaped forward, grabbed the bag, and started running away, zig zagging through the trees, just as Jack threw himself at

Tarzan's arm, causing him to drop his gun. Dan picked it up and threw it away into the trees.

"What are you doing?" Jack demanded. "We could have used that!"

"Just a reflex," Dan said.

Angus started running into the forest after Silvia. Stephen sprinted after him. Dan threw himself on Tarzan, and Siggy jumped on his back, trying to wrestle him to the ground.

"Have you been following me this whole time?" he yelled at her as he tried to get her off his back. "I can't believe you're so two-faced!"

"What about you, you cheat, hitting on me the whole time I had a boyfriend."

"Well Tarzan isn't much of a boyfriend."

"His name is Al!"

They heard a scream farther in the woods. Jack landed a punch on Tarzan's jaw. Dan wrenched out of Siggy's grasp, and they went charging in the direction of Silvia's scream.

They found her in the grasp of—

"The Asian!" Dan gasped. The man was holding a knife to her throat. Stephen was out cold on the ground in front of them.

"I wish people would stop saying that," the man said in a thick Scottish accent. "It sounds so racist."

"You're Monty Eu."

"Now therrre you go again," the man said frowning. "I've got yer niece and yeh just talk smack. It's Montagu, Euan Montagu."

"Then you're—"

"He's my son," Angus said. He was bent over and breathing heavily; sweat was pouring off his face.

"What about Tarzan?"

"Al? He's—"

"My brother from another mother," Euan said. Everyone looked towards him, eyebrows raised. "Literally."

"My first marriage didn't take," Angus explained. He pulled out a handkerchief and wiped his brow.

"Wonder why," Dan muttered.

"Hand Al the treasure, now, please. We are the descendants of Hugh Montagu and it's our birthright."

Jack scoffed, "It's not your birthright if you stole it in the first place."

"That," Angus said, "is also our family birthright."

"What? Piracy? Hugh Junior *was* a pirate, wasn't he?" Dan said. "I knew it!"

"Family legend says as much."

Dan stepped forward, forgetting the precariousness of their situation in the quest for knowledge. "What happened to him?"

"As far as I can tell…" Angus said, again wiping his brow, "do you have any water in that bag of yours?"

"Oh sure." Dan pulled out a bottle of water and gave it to Angus.

"—after he left St. Kitts he jumped onto a pirate ship. He had some kids who went into the family business and then died. His son took his family back to Barbados, perhaps to find the treasure, but he disappeared."

"Do you think he ever sailed up this far, you know, doing his pirate thing?"

"There's a possibility." Angus took another sip of water and wiped his brow.

"Are you okay?" Dan asked. But Angus just waved the question away.

"Dad," Euan said, "can we maybe hurry this up a bit? Al, why don't you—"

Al punched Dan in the face; he dropped his bag and fell to his knees. Al picked up the bag while Siggy and Jack helped lift Dan to his feet.

"Not exactly what I was going to say," Euan said, "but just as effective." He pushed Silvia forward towards Dan, when the sound of guns being cocked made them all freeze.

"Now what?" Dan muttered.

Maria stepped out from behind a tree. "Hello, Dan," she said. Two more people stepped out from behind the trees, their guns trained on the group. It was the bald man and the man with dreadlocks from Carolina.

"They're with you?" Dan asked incredulously. "You set me up!" He was outraged. "I cannot believe this!" he continued. "First Siggy and now you. What is it with women?"

Miracle

He gestured to Angus and Maria. "Which one of you tried to shoot Silvia in the head?"

Tarzan lifted his hand. "That was me," he said calmly. "I was just getting her attention. If I wanted to kill her"—he shrugged—"I would have."

Dan gave him an annoyed look and turned towards Maria; he pointed his finger at her. "I was going to fly back to Barbados and take you to Champers again, try to finish the date. You'd have the Cajun blackened dolphin—"

"Dolphin!" Silvia said.

"—and I'd have the Bajan flying fish."

"Dan," Maria said dismissively, "you are taking this much too much to heart."

The rest of the people watched the two as if they were in a tennis match.

"So, tell me, Maria, what have you been up to since I left Carolina with my face the size of a football? How is the real estate market? We still haven't had that moonlight swim yet, are you still game for that? Did you close any of those South Carolina prospects?"

She pursed her lips. "I've been quite busy, since you left."

"I see."

"Well, I am very tired and looking forward to a nice dip in the ocean when I get home. So"—she gestured to everyone—"let's do this a little quicker."

"No, Al," Dan said, "don't give her anything till she tells us why. What does any of this mean to you? A payday? Have you been passing information to Angus Montagu the whole time?" he demanded.

"Now stop right there—" Angus cut in.

Dan started pacing back and forth. "It's difficult to come to this conclusion, but it seems the most logical conclusion. You knew about my early research at the archives and the museum. And then my room was robbed. You knew I was going to South Carolina, and my visit to Goose Creek, and then I was attacked. You had me beat up!"

"I did not," she snapped back. "If you weren't trying to play the hero, nothing would have happened to you."

"In each case," he went on, "you were the only person who knew."

"Oh, I think your family knew and your friends. Plenty of people—"

"They are people I trust. What gives? Is this all just a game to you?"

"A game? A game!" She was so angry, she was crying. "My family came from Coral Castle. *Your* ancestor William sold a fourteen-year-old child to be a sex slave. To be abused. To be used."

"Look Maria, William Graham of Coral Castle was not my ancestor, I am descended from the Devon Farm Grahams."

Dan's anger cooled immediately. The man with the dreadlocks kept his gun trained on them, but moved in to give her a one-armed hug. "No, she said softly to him. "Tio, I must finish this." She tried to gather herself. "I thought I was descended from the union of an early owner of Coral Castle plantation, a Graham—"

"—William," Dan said, stricken. Silvia moved next to him to grab his hand.

"—but as you researched, I realized the timing wasn't right. In 1715, William was already—"

"Sean Mulroney!"

"—dead. Yes, Sean Mulroney. A man without a soul. He had his way with her many times and got her pregnant. He was twisted and cruel. Your ancestor Robert must have known this."

"As a result of slavery," Tio said, picking up the thread, "my family has had a vendetta with the Graham family, as they were treated very badly in the slavery days."

"William was a good man," Dan insisted.

"He owned slaves. He enabled Sean Mulroney."

"To make it worse," Maria continued, "my female slave ancestor was kicked off the plantation after my "mulatto" ancestor was born, and the family was left to fend for themselves."

"And that is why you will give us the treasure," the bald man said. Everyone seemed a little surprised that he spoke. He straightened his arms and cocked the gun.

Then Angus made a funny noise and dropped to his knees. At first Dan thought he'd somehow been shot, but his face had turned the colour of cold porridge and he was clutching his chest.

"Oh no," Silvia cried out. "He's having a heart attack."

Miracle

"Dad!" cried Al and Euan. They surged forward to help him, feeling helpless themselves. Maria knelt to look at his face. Tio and the bald man stood unmoving.

Maria hissed at them, "*Ayúdalo.*"

Grudgingly, they stepped forward. It turned out they were paramedics. Tio gave his phone to Maria and said, "Call 9-1-1; he's having a heart attack."

"Hey, that's my phone!" Dan complained. "Hey, you were the two paramedics on the beach with Mercedes too! She's your sister isn't she?"

"Uncle Dan," Silvia said, scandalized, "this isn't the place for that."

The rest was a blur of chest pumping. Tio and his brother, whose name turned out to be Eduardo, saved the day. Without their help, the surgeon said Angus wouldn't still be alive. In all the busyness and fear, the St. Cuthbert Treasure was forgotten. Not by Dan, he grabbed it and held onto it tightly and never let the bag out of his sight.

But something happened in the near death: life trumped hatred and vengeance. Perhaps the St. Cuthbert Treasure was making one more miracle.

CHAPTER FOURTEEN
Red, Red Wine

Harbour Lights Night Club on Bay Street was as usual full of tourists of all shapes, sizes, and colours. It was on the south coast and used to be opposite the Bay Mansion, an old Barbados plantation house. Dan used to ride past it every day on his way to school and wonder what it would be like, living on a plantation.

Harbour Lights claimed to be one of the most famous party locations in Barbados. Their grill served up Caribbean delicacies such as Mahi Mahi, flying fish, Bajan fish cakes, macaroni pie, calypso rice, black bean and corn salad, vegetarian dishes, and much more.

A large group sat at wooden tables on the patio under the strings of festive lights and swaying coconut trees. Aunt Mary and Jessica were there to celebrate and Stephen and John as well as the Montagus.

"A toast!" Dan said. "To warm Barbadian nights. To enemies turned friends. And to Angus's good health."

"To Angus." They all raised their glasses of rum punch. Then he called out, "Go on everybody! Eat! I hear they've got Bajan fish cakes."

Then the band struck up.

It had been six months since the day they'd found the St. Cuthbert Treasure relics , nearly lost them, and saved a life. When Dan thought back to that day, what struck him the most was that, faced with someone in true crisis, their differences and feuds had seemed to melt away.

The ambulance had airlifted Angus and family to the Nanaimo Regional General Hospital. By then Stephen had come to and was very peeved he'd missed the action. The paramedics brought him along for the ride to check him for a concussion.

"This must have been some party," one of the paramedics said.

Then, they gathered at the Surf Lodge and Pub to talk through everything. They decided not to open the burlap-wrapped treasure until they'd joined the Montagus. Three days later, they were sitting around Angus, who was propped up in bed. His wife, Lynette, was fussing over his blankets.

Dan held up the burlap package and a pair of white gloves. He handed both to Angus.

"It's only fitting that you unwrap it," Dan said. "You've waited your whole life for it."

"And nearly lost it because of it," the Scotsman said. But he put on the gloves and began to unwrap the burlap. All eyes were on his hands. The burlap finally gave way to reveal an ornate silver canister, tarnished with age.

"I knew it," Dan said. "A tea caddy."

It was locked, but it was a fairly primitive, old-fashioned lock. Eduardo pulled out two little tools from his wallet—"Don't ask," he said and he reached for the caddy and soon they heard a click. He handed the caddy back to Angus.

"Here goes," Angus said. He opened the lid. On top were four rings. He carefully took them out and placed them on his blanket. The rings were made of thick bands of gold with large, colourful uncut gems.

"Imagine. These were once on the fingers of a saint," he said.

He reached back into the caddy and carefully pulled out six bracelets, laying them on his blanket. They were made of rough-cut stones. One looked like a bracelet rosary.

"He would have prayed with this."

There was one more thing in the caddy; it was wrapped in old linen. Angus carefully unwrapped the material. It was a cross, about six inches long, inlaid with jewels.

"What a beautiful cross," Silvia said.

"Not just any cross," Angus said. "A pectoral cross. He would have worn this over his heart."

"They say the pectoral cross could have a relic inside it, either a relic of a saint or a fragment of the True Cross," Euan said. Silvia looked impressed;

he shrugged and added, "I learned all about this saint stuff since I was a kid."

Angus ran his fingers over the cross, gently probing. His fingers finally stopped and he pushed on a piece of it. One of the jewels popped open. Inside, was a sliver of wood that had become petrified with age.

Everyone looked on with awe.

After that, they had contacted Durham Castle and it took some time to negotiate the return of the relics and get the reward. It involved a trip out to England. But finally, the St. Cuthbert Treasure relics were home, and Angus could fulfill his plan to help descendants of the Scottish prisoners from the Battle of Dunbar. They also funded a TV program on Irish and Scottish prisoners who became indentured servants, with the help of the Scottish POW organization.

Now the band was playing one of Dan's favourite reggae songs: *Red, Red Wine*.

"Let's dance, Maria," Dan said, and with a flourish, he pulled her onto the dance floor. At first, he was a bit slow at getting into the groove, but once the rum punch started flowing into his veins, he quickly relaxed and began winding his hips to the music.

The live entertainment for the evening featured three Caribbean bands, fire-eaters, limbo dancers, and captivating dancers. Back in Vancouver, a live Caribbean band would sometimes come to town and play in the Commodore Ballroom, including, years ago, the Merrymen. He'd always tell anyone who would listen that the lead singer grew up on Worthing Beach with him in Barbados.

One of their selections, *Beautiful Barbados*, was one of his folk Caribbean favourites. He told his two daughters that when he died, at his Celebration of Life, he wanted two pieces of music played: *Red, Red Wine* and *Beautiful Barbados*. If they could squeeze in a third song, then *Lady in Red*. That way he'd be jiving into heavenly living, right to the end.

Dan spun Maria and pulled her in; they laughed as they moved together. But, it was different between them now; their feelings had changed, moving from passion to protection. So, when a tall, handsome, Spanish-looking guy cut in and, ignoring Dan, said "Hi, Maria," Dan wasn't mad like he once would be. He did, however, eye him up and down.

Maria looked a bit embarrassed. "Dan, this is Max. He just returned to Barbados from America."

Dan gave him a smile. "Hi Max. Nice to meet you."

"Max, Dan is a Barbadian. He's doing some family research and wants me to help him find a condo in Barbados."

Dan figured he was more than just a guy from the office.

He leaned in and said, "See all those guys at that table? Especially the big hairy one. We all love Maria and would be devastated if you break her heart." He looked Max in the eye. "You understand."

"A hundred percent, sir."

Dan winked at him, kissed Maria, and left the crowd to go walk on the beach.

He felt so relieved; he had not only been successful in finding the stolen artifacts of the St. Cuthbert Treasures, he was helping the descendants of the Scottish prisoners from the battle of Dunbar, and had also found the Spanish treasure, which would allow him to do all the beneficial things that he wanted to do personally: help his Aunt Mary and his sister Jessica and her family and help local Barbadian people with the best gift, education. By a strange twist of fate, just like him moving from one of England's oldest colonies, Barbados, to British Columbia, his treasure hunt had moved from Barbados to one of England's newest colonies, before it became part of Canada, the same British Columbia,

It was Dan's last day in Barbados; he had said goodbye to Aunt Mary, Jessica, Silvia, Jack, and Leo earlier and thanked them all for their help. He would take care of them. He went out for a swim at his traditional time of 4.30 pm; it was in front of where his grandfather's house used to be, which had now been replaced with new condos.

The beach in front had shrunk, the invading sea now crashed against the seawall at high tide, more evidence of climate change. The invasion of the Sargassum seaweed from Brazil was supposedly caused by the cutting of the Brazilian forests, and the resulting flood of fertilizers and pesticides into the rivers, and then the sea.

Even where the weed had moved on, the seawater was brown.

He sat on the empty beach and listened to the sound of waves lapping on the white sand, and the waving coconut trees above him.

Through an old Swiss banking contact, Dan had been successful in selling the Spanish gold offshore in Hong Kong with the proceeds accessible in the Cayman Islands.

He also remembered what the hundred-year-old sugar planter had said to him about how the English had mistreated slave families at Emancipation, with the slave owners getting all the emancipation payouts and the Black families getting nothing. He found a way to share a portion of the new wealth from the Spanish gold with the descendants of the slaves his family had owned through the area schools. It was still in process, but everyone felt good about it.

He thought that doing something like this for the descendants of the slaves at Coral Castle and Devon Farm just might start the ball rolling in Barbados reparations, helping the issue get off the ground practically, instead of just being talked about.

The Montagu clan gave some of their reward money to the descendants of Scottish soldiers who were transported to the American colonies after the Battle of Dunbar. The Scots POW Association helped look after that.

From the proceeds of selling the Spanish treasure, Dan gave money to schools teaching descendants of the slaves and indentured servants from the two Graham plantations and the poor whites in Martins Bay. He gave money to provide better facilities, more structures, more computers, and books, and to provide bursaries and scholarships for further education for their children. Primary schools in Barbados could always use extra help.

Dan funded new projects that would clean up the environment and support sustainable development, green energy, and climate change. Things like converting bagasse, or sugar cane waste, into ethanol and other valuable products like xylose for diabetic chewing gum. A modular housing technology that built small houses cheaply from local waste wood, especially useful after hurricane destruction. A flower and fruit preservation technology from Vancouver that would preserve flowers so they could be shipped from Barbados to the Dutch flower auction daily. He even turned the Sargassum seaweed problem into an opportunity by funding a technology converting the weed into garden fertiliser just as his father had done with seamoss in the old days.

In the early days, when they were bandying around what to do with the money, Dan had said, "What I think I want to do is become an angel investor and put money into new companies that make a difference to the environment and slow down climate change." Now he spent part of his time in West Vancouver, taking the time to also visit friends and family. The other part of his year he spent in Barbados.

He played an interview for his family, thinking they'd get a kick out of it, and it was also in the local *Barbados Nation* newspaper:

"An anonymous Barbados-born person, now living overseas, is the head of a private corporation that has made a significant donation to the three local schools that were in communities where the donor's family had owned land historically, the monies will be used to improve the quality of education these communities receive and for scholarships."

The school principals had cooperated, and now it was up to them to follow through.

"Hopefully the public will get involved," Dan had said, "and the parents of the students in the community schools will ensure that the monies flow as intended."

It was later reported in the local press that three schools had received about $500,000 each in local currency from this anonymous donor.

From where he sat, his mind too full of thoughts to understand them, he could see the whole length of the beach where he'd grown up and made so many memories. It hadn't changed much, except for the sea invading and taking over the beach.

He could recount all the houses, their house names, and which family had lived there. He watched the rocking of the anchored boats at their moorings, as the waves rolled in from the reef. Memories came flooding back and he couldn't understand why he felt so … sad. He went to the Carib Beach bar.

"Hey," a voice called out, "is that Dan Graham, the ladies' man from Worthing Beach?"

Dan looked up, "Tommy! How the heck are you, my friend? Glad you could make it."

"Doing great. Arlene and I are doing a trial getting-back-together."

Dan smiled. "You look happy."

Red, Red Wine

"Yeah, I think I am."

Dan nodded his head. "You can go on in; I'll be there in a minute." He looked back out to the rolling waves. "Just being a little nostalgic."

"Sure, um, I hope you're okay with this," Tommy said, "but I invited some people."

"Arlene?"

"No. Some old friends.

At that moment two men arrived; one was Stephen and the other was Martindale or Marty, who lived in a house on Worthing Beach. Marty was an expert on finding lost coins and jewellery on the beach. Stephen told them, " the leader of the Merrymen regrets that he couldn't make it, but he is at Government house receiving a music award. However he assures us that Millie did come back from Brazil." *Millie gone to Brazil* was one of their favourite Merrymen's songs.

"Good to have wunna all here back on the beach, a reunion of old beach bums, I got some good news, my PSA is now below one, and all my scans were clear, no more cancer."

"Let's all drink to that," Tommy said, "I guess you are back in the saddle."

"Just have to find a horse now," Dan laughed.

"Well I think you will find one sooner than you think," Tommy joked.

Later, after they talked about old times on Worthing Beach and the others had left, Tommy picked up his phone and soon after, a woman walked up the beach towards them.

The woman was tall, with a full, shapely figure. Her lush hair bounced around her shoulders as she walked. She sure looked familiar. As she came closer, the woman smiled and said softly, "Dan."

He felt time slip. It might have been thirty-one years ago, on the same beach, in front of his grandfather's old cottage, saying goodbye to someone that he cared for. She had dared him to write a poem about them, about their affair. The sun was now dropping below the horizon, with that brilliant green splash it makes in the tropics, as it suddenly disappears below the horizon. It was almost the same time of day.

He had held her close and kissed her lips, and then, he had walked away. Twenty-four hours later he was on an Air Canada flight on his way to Montreal. When he wrote the poem he was nineteen years old living in an apartment on Lincoln Avenue in bitterly cold Montreal in winter. She looked just as she always had, although with a few tints of grey.

> Was it so good to cross the sea
> And leave my love so far from me?
> Though never could she be my wife,
> Yet with her I would share my life.
> I glimpsed when first I held her hand,
> With shoeless feet we skipped on sand,
> She smiled at me and coyly said,
> Dan, secret love, with you I'll wed.
> I loved her charm, her lips, her eyes,
> As we embraced under moonlit skies,
> The greatest moment of my dreams,
> My love was splitting at the seams.
> 'Twas on that beach that I first swam,
> Held in the arms of Dad and Mom,
> Where I had passed my boyhood age,
> Where now I felt love's spreading rage.
> But love in secret cannot last,
> And leads to times of loveless fast,
> I feared my love and I would sin,
> I left my love and took to wing.
> And I left my dearest island home,
> And the land of the Maple I 'gan to roam,
> And though my love is far away,
> I think of her each night and day.
> I see her as she coyly beckons,
> Me to come home, make up lost seconds,
> Perhaps one day she will be free,
> And consent to share her life with me.

Patricia put her hand on Dan's shoulder in an affectionate way. "Do you remember when the sea was much farther out than it is now?" she asked.

"Yes," he replied. "Do you remember the twin boys who used to walk along the beach here with a throwing net to catch fish? I believe that they were related to Tommy."

"Do you remember the fishing boats with sails that used to be anchored just off the beach here?"

He didn't know how to handle Patricia and, though they conversed easily, he felt there was no turning back. A lot of water had flowed under their bridge. Suddenly, just like thirty-one years ago, Dan had to get out of there, so he stood up, said goodbye, and went back down the beach.

He was almost to the end of the beach when he thought he heard a small voice in his ear, *"Turn towards your future."*

Patricia was still standing there, like a beacon in the early moonlight. Suddenly he was running down the beach towards her. She stretched out her arms in welcome.

CHAPTER FIFTEEN
Sleep Well, Angel

With each wave hitting the rock, seagulls and other birds screamed and, temporarily dislodged from their homes, flew up to avoid the water. They milled around, making shrill noises, until they could return to their little nests. The Ramier pigeons spread their wings to dry in the hot sun.

As the waves reached closer to shore they become smaller, and smaller, until just a small body of water rushed up onto the beach, carrying with it the kelp, and other assorted sea moss, flotsam, and jetsam.

The beach was now covered with all kinds of birds, running to and fro, including little sandpipers moving around quickly on their two little stork-like legs, picking tasty nutrients out of the water.

The seagulls fought amongst themselves for the little crabs that washed up with the incoming tide.

Dan stood by the cliff-face, looking out at the view, then he got in his car and drove back to Coral Castle.

He shifted the vase of flowers in his hand and then went over and placed it in front of the gravestone. It was ornately carved with a beautiful statue of an angel with fierce eyes looking over the graves as if protecting them: William Graham, Isabel Graham, and Joseph Graham.

It was Alison who had picked the design. And it was Alison who inadvertently solved the mystery of little Joseph. She and Ben had bought Coral Castle and were going to turn it into a bed and breakfast. She was taking Dan through the grounds at Coral Castle, showing him how far the work had progressed on the grounds. She wanted to convert the boiling house to a rental.

"I see an open concept, with wide sweeping windows on this side, so you get a view of the mill," she said. "And don't you just love this old stone? I think we should use salvaged local wood for the interior details." Then she led him by hand back out, pulling him towards the mill.

"And I've had this stroke of brilliance," she continued, "just last night as I was lying in bed." She and Ben were staying in a small bedroom at the top of the house under the eaves so she could oversee the renovations in progress. "I was turning over what to do with the mill in my mind, when I suddenly saw a chapel. With the fans restored, why, from a distance, it looks like a church."

A chill rushed up Dan's spine. *He lies without and looks up to God.*

"Quick, Alison," he said, "grab some shovels. I know where Joseph is."

Not only did she grab shovels, but Ben and half a dozen workers as well. To the worried calls of "Be careful," "Dig gently," "It's got to be here in the bushes or he'd be seen," they looked for Joseph.

They found his little body with tattered remnants of his linen night shirt surrounding him. Around his wrist were two prayer bead bracelets. They had a name engraved on each: "William" and "Isabel." His head was turned up "as if looking up to God," Dan said, tears filling his eyes.

So they had finally reunited Joseph with his family and buried them together.

Family is a precious thing, Dan thought. He'd decided he could share his life, with his friends in Vancouver, his daughters, his family in Barbados, and his new fiancée, Patricia. He came to understand that you can never know what will be befall you today, tomorrow, but that doesn't mean you should turn away from life.

He patted the gravestone and looked out over the blue Caribbean waters far in the distance. *What a wonderful way to end the day.*

"Sleep well, little Joseph. I'll visit again tomorrow."

APPENDIX 1
The Island of Barbados

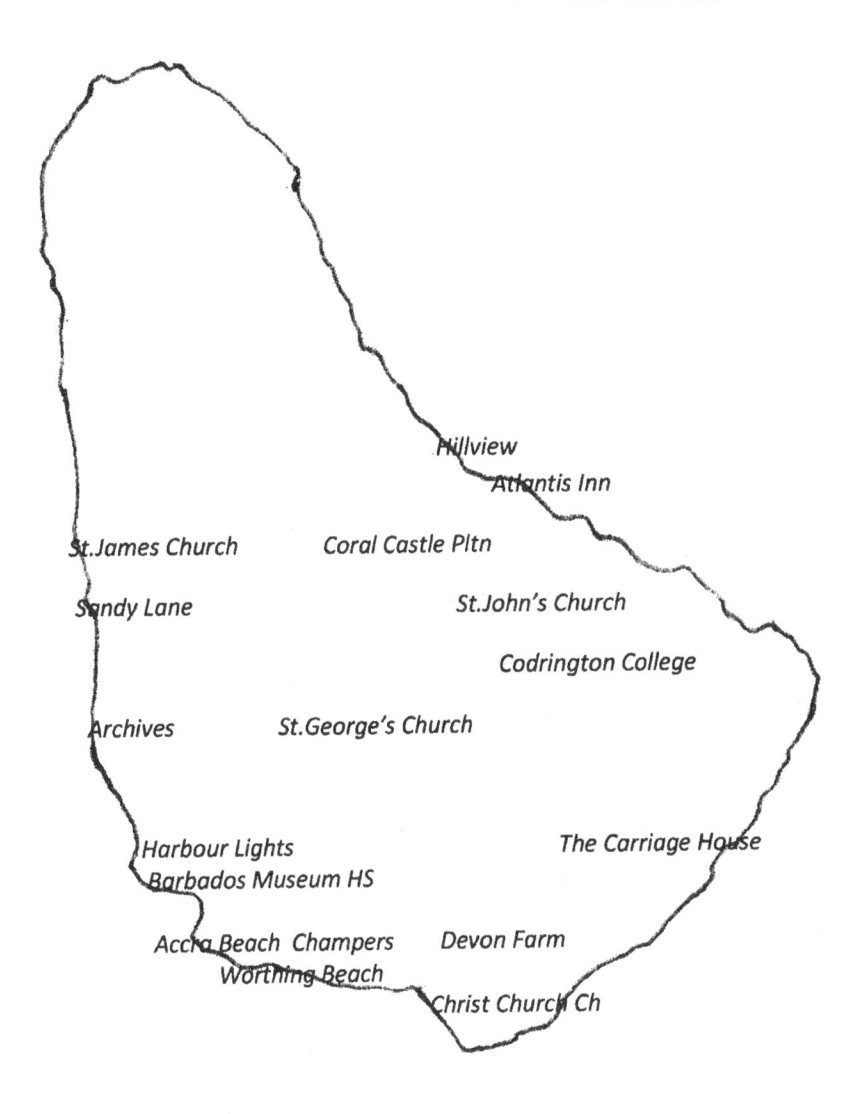

- Hillview
- Atlantis Inn
- St.James Church
- Coral Castle Pltn
- Sandy Lane
- St.John's Church
- Codrington College
- Archives
- St.George's Church
- Harbour Lights
- The Carriage House
- Barbados Museum HS
- Accra Beach
- Champers
- Devon Farm
- Worthing Beach
- Christ Church Ch

APPENDIX 2
Family Trees

Family Name				Location
Graham	Robert/Joane Devon Farm D.1677		William/Mary Coral Castle Pltn D.1680	Barbados
Son	Robert/Sarah D.1707		William/ Isabel D.1706	Barbados
	Robert Son –		Joseph Son 1700-1710	Barbados
Descendant	Dan B.1970		Jessica Sister	Barbados West Van

Relics of a Saint: A Barbados Mystery

Montagu	Hugh D.1680	Prisoner Indentured Servant		Durham Barbados
Son	Hugh/ Maureen B.1671	Militiaman		Barbados St.Kitts
Son	Phillippe D.1735	Pirate		West Indies
Mulroney	Sean D.1738	Lawyer	Hannah Elizabeth Thomas	Barbados South Carolina
Son	Sean D.1745			Barbados South Carolina
Son	Sean D.1800			Ontario Province
Son	Sean D.1815			Ontario Province

FAMILY TREES

Son	Robert Sean D.1848			Ontario Province
Son	Sean D.1896			Victoria City
Son	Sean D.1926			Victoria City
Son	Sean D.1980			Gabriola Island
Son	Sean D.2000			Gabriola Island
Son	Sean D.2020			Gabriola Island

BIBLIOGRAPHY

American Justice pamphlet. *The present state of justice in the American Plantations, and particularly in the Island of Barbados; which being the best modeled of the plantations, the condition of the rest may be thereby conjectured.* 1702.

American Philosophical Society. *To Benjamin Franklin from Sir Philip Gibbes, 5 Jan. 1778.* Letter from Sir Philip Gibbes. National Archives. https://founders.archives.gov/documents/Franklin/01-25-02-0341. also franklinpapers.org/framedVolumes.jsp?vol=23&page=281a

Archaeology International –A late Saladoid site at Hillcrest Barbados, Journal of the Barbados Museum and Historical Society 1993 JP Prewett,

Barbados Integrated Government. "Department of Archives." https://www.gov.bb/Departments/archives.

Barbados Museum and Historical Society. https://www.facebook.com/barbadosmuseum/.

BC Parks. "Gabriola Sands Provincial Park." http://bcparks.ca/explore/parkpgs/gabriola_sands/.

Beckles, Hilary McD. *Bussa: the 1816 Barbados Revolution.* Barbados: Barbados Museum and Historical Society, and University of the West Indies, 1998.

Brandow, James C., ed. *Omitted chapters from Hotten's original lists of persons of quality and others who went from Great Britain to the American plantations, 1600-1700*. Baltimore: Genealogical Publishing Company, 1983.

British Library. "British Library Acquires the St. Cuthbert Gospel—the earliest intact European book." https://www.bl.uk/press-releases/2012/april/british-library-acquires-the-st-cuthbert-gospel--the-earliest-intact-european-book.

Campbell, P.F. *Some Early Barbadian History*. Barbados: n.p., 1993.

Champers. http://champersrestaurant.com/.

Codrington College. http://www.codrington.org/site/index.php.

Davy, John. *The West Indies before and since slave emancipation: comprising the windward and leeward islands military command; founded on notes and observations collected during a three years' residency*. London: Frank Cass and Company, 1971.

Dictionary of Canadian Biography. "Douglas, Sir James." http://www.biographi.ca/en/bio/douglas_james_10E.html.

Dobson, David. *Barbados and Scotland, links 1627-1877*. Baltimore: Clearfield, 2005.

Duell, Charles. *Middleton Place: a phoenix still rising*. Charleston: Middleton Place Foundation, 2011.

Equiano, Olaudah. *The interesting narrative of the life of Olaudah Equiano, or Gustavus Vassa, the African. Written by himself*. London, 1789. Chapter V.

BIBLIOGRAPHY

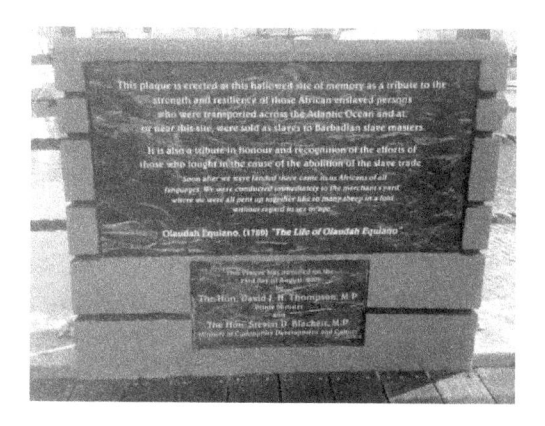

Slave plaque in Barbados referring to Olaudah Equiano.

Free tours by foot. "Historic Charleston: a self-guided tour." https://freetoursbyfoot.com/historic-charleston-self-guided-tour/.

Gabriola Museum. "Gabriola's history timeline." https://gabriolamuseum.org/connections-and-resources/gabriola-island-timeline/

Gabriola Caves. https://www.inspirock.com/canada/gabriola-island/malaspina-galleries-a1182612193

Handler, Jerome S. *The Unappropriated People: freedmen in the slave society of Barbados.* Jamaica: University of the West Indies Press, 2009.

Harbour Lights Barbados. https://www.harbourlightsbarbados.com/.

Harlow, Vincent T. *Christopher Codrington 1668-1710.* Oxford: Clarendon Press, 1928.

Hoffius, Stephen G. *South Carolina and Barbados connection, selections from the South Carolina Historical Magazine.* Charleston: Home House Press, 2011.

Laurie, Peter. *The Barbadian Rum Shop*. London: Macmillan Education, 2001.

Library and Archives Canada. "Censuses." Government of Canada. https://www.bac-lac.gc.ca/eng/census/Pages/census.aspx.

—"Land Petitions of Upper Canada, 1763-1865." https://www.bac-lac.gc.ca/eng/discover/land/land-petitions-upper-canada-1763-1865/Pages/land-petitions-upper-canada.aspx.

—"The Pacific Coast." Government of Canada. https://www.bac-lac.gc.ca/eng/discover/exploration-settlement/pathfinders-passageways/Pages/pacific-coast.aspx.

www.liberiapastandpresent.org/Barclay/Arthur.htm

Ligon, Richard Gent. *A True and Exact History of the Island of Barbados*. First published London, 1657. London: Frank Cass and Company, 1970.

Lumsden, May. *The Barbados–American Connection*. Texas: Layne Publishing, 1982.

Malaspina Galleries.https://www.inspirock.com/canada/gabriola-island/malaspina-galleries-a1182612193

Marryat, Frederick. *Peter Simple*. London: Saunders and Otley, 1834.

Metaldetector.com. "Deep seeking 2 box." https://www.metaldetector.com/hobby-metal-detectors/deep-seeking-2-box.

Nelson, William. *The American Tory*. 1961. Reprint. Boston: Northeastern University Press, 1992.

O'Callaghan, Sean. *To Hell or Barbados: the ethnic cleansing of Ireland*. Kerry: Brandon Books, 2001.

BIBLIOGRAPHY

Poyer, John. *The History of Barbados from the First Discovery of the Island, in the Year 1605, till the Accession of Lord Seaforth, 1801.* London: 1808.

Sabatini, Rafael. *Captain Blood.* New York: Houghton Mifflin, 1922.

Sadgrove, Michael. *Durham Cathedral: the Shrine of St. Cuthbert.* Norwich: Jarrold Publishing, 2005.

Sheppard, Jill. *The "redlegs" of Barbados: their origins and history.* New York: KTO Press, 1977.

South Carolina Department of Archives and History. https://www.scencyclopedia.org/sce/entries/south-carolina-department-of-archives-and-history

Stockton, Robert P. "Historic Resources of Berkeley County South Carolina." Berkeley County: Berkeley County Historical Society and South Carolina Department of Archives and History, 1990. http://nationalregister.sc.gov/SurveyReports/HC08002.pdf.

Sullivan, Anthony. "Britain's War against the Slave Trade. Frontline Books 2020.

The Atlantis Historic Inn. https://www.atlantishotelbarbados.com/.

The Crane. https://www.thecrane.com/.

Tripadvisor. "Malaspina Galleries." https://www.tripadvisor.ca/Attraction_Review-g499132-d4805548-Reviews-or15-Malaspina_Galleries-Gabriola_Island_British_Columbia.html.

United Empire Loyalists' Association of Canada. "The United Empire Loyalists." http://www.uelac.org/.

Wide Sargasso Sea. Directed by John Duigan. Adaptation of 1966 novel of the same name by Jean Rhys. United States: New Line Cinema, 1993.

Wigfield, W. McDonald. *The Monmouth rebels: 1685*. Gloucester: Allan Sutton Publishing Limited, 1985.

Wilson, Bruce G. "Loyalists in Canada." Canadian Encyclopedia. April 2, 2009. https://www.thecanadianencyclopedia.ca/en/article/loyalists.

Wikipedia. "Battle of Dunbar (1650)." https://en.wikipedia.org/wiki/Battle_of_Dunbar_(1650).

—"Chase Vault." https://en.wikipedia.org/wiki/Chase_Vault.

—"Ferdinand Paleologus." https://en.wikipedia.org/wiki/Ferdinand_Paleologus.

— "Joe Fortes." https://en.wikipedia.org/wiki/Joe_Fortes.

—"Richard Clement Moody." https://en.wikipedia.org/wiki/Richard_Clement_Moody.

Woodard, Colin. *The Republic of Pirates: being the true and surprising story of the Caribbean pirates and the man who brought them down*. London: Houghton Mifflin Harcourt, 2007.